"You're a very distracting woman..."

The kiss was glorious. A stroke of his tongue at the front of her upper palate, a nip on her bottom lip. Then Daniel pressed against her as he thrust into her mouth, their rhythm perfectly in sync, possessive, unguarded and hot as hell.

Lisa moaned when he brought his hand between them and cupped her breast.

"Shh," he whispered. "Don't make a sound."

She was so wired, she could probably start electrical fires. The door might be locked, but that didn't mean they wouldn't be discovered. Public sex wasn't her thing, but this? Her breathlessness was a sure sign that she was up for the challenge.

He was quicker than her. He'd opened the top button of her jeans, and he was starting to push them down her hips. A moment later he gave each cheek a squeeze she'd remember for a while.

Quickly she had his belt open, button undone and zipper down.

"The rest is up to you, Dr. Cassidy."

D1456383

Dear Reader,

Intrigue Me is the sixth book of the It's Trading Men! miniseries, and I've enjoyed writing them so much. But another miniseries has been calling me, so this will be the last of the trading card novels, at least for a while.

My heroine, Lisa, is a wounded ex-cop who's now an undercover private eye. The hero, Daniel, is the Hot Guy she's investigating while he's working at a Bronx free clinic. They think it's just a physical attraction. It can't turn into anything more. Daniel doesn't even know her real name! But the best laid plans...

Just thinking about their rocky road from no-strings nights to life-changing confessions, and how they help each other grow and open up to love gives me goosebumps.

Some books just get under my skin, and Daniel and Lisa's story is one of those. I hope it becomes one of those for you, too.

You can write to me at joleigh@joleigh.com, or find me on Twitter @Jo_Leigh.

Sincerely,

Jo Leigh

Jo Leigh

—

Intrigue Me

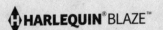

HHARLEQUIN® BLAZE™

Recycling programs
for this product may
not exist in your area.

ISBN-13: 978-0-373-79848-3

Intrigue Me

Copyright © 2015 by Jolie Kramer

HARLEQUIN®
www.Harlequin.com

Printed in U.S.A.

Jo Leigh is from Los Angeles and always thought she'd end up living in Manhattan. So how did she end up in Utah in a tiny town with a terrible internet connection being bossed around by a house full of rescued cats and dogs? What the heck, she says, predictability is boring. Jo has written more than forty-five novels for Harlequin. Visit her website at joleigh.com or contact her at joleigh@joleigh.com.

Books by Jo Leigh

HARLEQUIN BLAZE

Coming Soon

Have Mercy

Ms. Match

Sexy Ms. Takes

Shiver

Hotshot

Choose Me

Have Me

Want Me

Lying in Bed

All the Right Moves

Seduce Me

Dare Me

COSMOPOLITAN RED-HOT READS FROM HARLEQUIN

Definitely Naughty

To get the inside scoop on Harlequin Blaze and its talented writers, be sure to check out blazeauthors.com.

All backlist available in ebook format.

Visit the Author Profile page at Harlequin.com for more titles

To my friends and colleagues,
Birgit, Debbi & Jill,
who are always there when I need them.
Thank you!

1

Lisa McCabe made sure no one was close enough to overhear her before she answered her brother's call. "What is it, Logan?"

"Where are you?" he asked. "Why are you whispering?"

"The Moss Street free clinic in the Bronx." She scanned the crowded waiting room again. "I'm checking out someone for our Hot Guys Trading Cards client."

"What about the Murphy divorce? I need that wrapped up today. They go to court next week."

"I typed up the report yesterday. The file's on your desk." She caught a glimpse of a tall man in scrubs and pulled a folded paper out of her purse.

"I don't see it."

"Did you check your in-box?" she asked. For a man who was on the verge of taking his security firm to a whole new level with the sting operation he was coordinating, her brother wasn't very organized with his paperwork. To be fair, he had more important things to be thinking about. And he definitely didn't need to be worrying about the divorce cases Lisa handled.

Her attention went to the photocopy of Dr. Daniel Cassidy's trading card while she absently listened to Logan shuffle papers.

Lisa had already deduced that the tall man in scrubs wasn't the object of her investigation—Cassidy was much better looking. His clean-cut dark hair made him look sharp and professional, but his eyes, the color of cognac, were just plain damn sexy.

If she belonged to the Hot Guys Trading Cards dating club she would've snapped up his card based on his looks alone, which was embarrassing to admit since she'd worked her butt off to prove she was more than a "pretty face." Still, the truth was, she'd do him in a minute. Or would have, in another life. She would never risk it now.

Her fingers traced the lips on the photocopy. They were full, yet masculine, with a hint of—

Logan muttered something.

She straightened, feeling as though she'd been caught in the adult section of the video store. "What?"

"Found it. Hold on while I give it a quick look."

"Sure." Lisa went back to studying the doctor's photo—more specifically his lips and how they were a perfect contrast to his square jaw. The image stopped at his shoulders but she'd bet the farm that the rest of his body was equally hot.

Her gaze went to the details on the reverse side of the trading card. Dr. Cassidy was looking to get married, preferred home-cooked meals to dining out, was passionate about using his skills to help people and had a great heart. All this according to Josephine Suarez, the woman who'd submitted his name and photo. If Cassidy himself had provided the information, it would've sounded creepy as hell. But that wasn't how Hot Guys Trading Cards worked.

Each of the women who belonged to the group was required to submit a photo of at least one guy she knew well enough to vouch for. Lisa had learned that not all of the guys knew they were being passed around and ogled. She wondered if Dr. Daniel Cassidy had given his approval.

"Good job. No typos this time, either," Logan said. "Now, what's this about the free clinic?"

"First, up-yours about the typos. Second, you didn't listen to a word I said last night, did you?"

Her brother grunted. "You didn't say anything about a free clinic."

A woman bumped Lisa's shoulder and she quickly slipped the paper back into her purse. "I didn't know he was working here until after we spoke," she said, keeping her voice low. "He shouldn't be, though. Not with his credentials. He's straight up Ivy League all the way. He could be bringing in beaucoup bucks, but instead he's volunteering full-time at a free clinic in the Bronx."

"So cynical. Maybe he's just a super nice guy."

She had every reason to be cynical and Logan knew it. But he was teasing her—part of his ongoing attempt to get her to lighten up. "Yeah, because so many of our clients hire us to investigate super nice guys."

"Fair point, but you realize this client didn't pay enough to merit a field visit," Logan said. "Hell, for what she paid, all you needed to do was look the guy up on Google and LinkedIn."

"He's not on LinkedIn."

"That's weird, but not weird enough to chase him down."

"So I'm thorough. Shoot me."

"Tempting." Logan's chair creaked. "Seriously, don't waste too much time on it," he said. "I think we might be getting another custody case tomorrow."

Lisa groaned. She hated those the most.

"Hey, it's the small, slimy stuff that helps pay the rent."

"True," she acknowledged. "Which is why I'm thinking about drumming up more Trading Card business."

"I thought those guys are already vetted."

"They are. I'm thinking there might be more gold diggers like Heather out there, though, who can't be bothered with a guy who doesn't make enough money." Lisa heard Logan shuffling more papers around and knew he wasn't listening. Understandable, since the human-trafficking case he was working on was much more interesting than what she was blathering on about. And yes, she was envious, and maybe that was a sign that she might not sleepwalk through the rest of her life. "I've gotta go," she told him. "We'll talk about it later."

"Sure. Good."

As soon as they disconnected, she sighed. Logan wasn't wrong about her wasting time. She knew damn well she was satisfying her own curiosity and calling it diligence. But by the same token, she was serious about trolling for more business for her brother's security firm at the Trading Card lunch meetings. She'd have to become a member, of course, which meant that she'd have to be recommended by someone in the club. Heather was the only member she knew, and then only as a client. But Lisa doubted that would matter to Heather. After all, she'd cheated. The rules let you choose one card at a time, but Lisa had received a photocopy of another doctor's card, as well.

Joining also meant she'd have to submit a guy to be put on a card. Her college friends had always called Logan a babe. She knew he wasn't in the market to date or get married. But if she checked the one-night-stand option? He might be game.

She put away her phone, and then made her way to the clinic's main waiting room. Lucky for her, someone vacated the green plastic chair next to where she was standing.

The clinic itself didn't seem very large. There was the overfilled waiting room where messy rows of mismatched chairs snaked around to fill as much space as possible. Down the hall were the examination rooms, and maybe a couple of offices from what she could glimpse.

In fact, the whole place had a patchwork feel to it. Graffiti covered the walls outside, except for the heavy glass door. It hadn't surprised her when she saw it was bullet-resistant. Inside, the walls were all painted in cheery pastels. One was plastered with pictures kids had drawn. It looked like a giant refrigerator door.

The people waiting to see a doctor were unsurprisingly diverse. Some were dressed in business attire, while others looked as if they were homeless. No one seemed bothered by the two young men covered in tattoos sitting among them.

From what she'd seen so far the staff was equally diverse. Only one physician was permanent, but they had quite a few volunteer specialists on rotation. There were also two full-time registered nurses, a physician's assistant and student nurses from the nearby hospital who came and went in order to accrue hours and experience. The same with medical students, although they were fewer in number. At least that was what it had said on the Moss Street Clinic website.

Lisa turned her attention to the African-American woman sitting beside her. Her eyes were sharp as they lit on every person in the room. Her tight lips, the small disapproving shakes of her head and her expressive eyebrows hid nothing.

Lisa figured if anyone knew the dirt on Dr. Cassidy, it would be her observant seat mate. "Excuse me," Lisa said. "I'm new to the clinic. Do you know anything about Dr. Cassidy?"

The woman turned to look at Lisa. She'd expected to get the once-over from her, but it still felt intrusive. "Why you askin'?"

"I've come to see him. For an exam."

"You mean a test? You one of them student doctors from Lincoln?"

"No. A patient."

Leaning back, the woman took in as much of Lisa as she could. "You don't look like nothin's wrong. You from the tabloids?"

"Uh, no. Why? Are the tabloids interested in Dr. Cassidy?"

"How should I know? What's your name?"

"Lisa Pine," she said, surprised when her mother's maiden name popped out. There was really no reason for her to use an alias. Though she kind of liked the idea. "And you are?"

The answer didn't come quickly. But finally she said, "Mrs. Alexis Washington."

Lisa held out her hand. "Nice to meet you. It's scary coming to a new place when you don't know anyone."

Mrs. Washington hesitated again, but eventually took Lisa's hand. "Where you live at?"

"I'm staying at the Days Inn by Yankee Stadium. Just for a while, though. I would have gone to Lincoln Hospital, but I heard someone talking about Dr. Cassidy. They said he's a neurologist. A really good one. And since I don't have any insurance…"

"You ask me, you come to the right place. I ain't been seen by Dr. Cassidy myself, but my neighbor Iris, she did. Said he was real nice. Listened to everything she told him. Didn't cut her off, or work on something else while she was talking, you know what I mean?"

"I do," Lisa said. "It's so difficult now. No doctors want

to listen. They just want you in and out, don't forget to pay when you leave."

Mrs. Washington laughed, and it was as if Lisa had been given a seal of approval. "You got that right." Then she leaned in closer and lowered her voice. "You're real pretty. You got something going on with one of them Yankees?"

It took Lisa a moment to make the connection to the Days Inn near the stadium. "No, Mrs. Washington. I don't. I'm single. No job. And a whole lot of headaches."

"Okay, now Iris, she came to see him because she was getting dizzy all the time. Almost fell over at the Burger King on Grand Concourse. Had to sit down. They gave her some ice water. Then she came straight here. Dr. Cassidy sent her over to get a CT scan—you know that's serious business—and they took her blood. They said she got some kind of disease that make you dizzy, and there ain't much to do 'bout it. But she's okay most the time."

"Sounds like he's a good doctor."

"Oh, yeah. You know, he don't get paid. Someone told me but I can't remember who. Not the woman who helps run the place, though. Eve is her name and she works for his daddy or his brother or somethin'. She been comin' down here to volunteer for a few years now, but she keeps her mouth shut, especially when it comes to Dr. Cassidy. He came a couple months back. I can't remember when. Too many things I got to worry 'bout in my own life."

Lisa nodded. "I hope you're not here for anything serious."

"Me, I'm fine. Strong as an ox. I'm here with my grandson." She glanced over to the corner where there was a small space for kids to play with books and toys. "Spider-Man today. All this year, pretty much. Here for a vaccination."

"Grandson? Wow, you don't look old enough to have grandchildren."

"I had 'em too young and they had 'em too young." Mrs. Washington leaned closer again, clearly pleased at the compliment. "They all nice here, for the most part. They don't have all that fancy equipment like in Manhattan, but if something bad happens with your headaches? They'll help find a way to get you right."

"Thank you. That makes me feel much better." Lisa reached into her purse and pulled out her cell phone. "Ah, it's my brother. Would you excuse me?" She stood and walked to a relatively quiet corner near the watercooler.

Logan hadn't actually called, but she wanted to get more than one opinion on Dr. Cassidy. She decided to focus on the staff next. There was a line at the reception desk, and the poor guy behind the counter had to answer the phones in between fielding questions. Lisa didn't mind waiting. From where she stood she could see down the hall toward the examination rooms. Occasionally, someone in scrubs or in a lab coat would appear and then enter another room. She'd hoped for a peek at Dr. Cassidy but hadn't had any luck so far. She would've known him right away...

"Can I help you?"

Lisa turned back to the reception desk. "I'm—"

Loud shouting pulled her attention back to the waiting room where two men were almost down each other's throats screaming so furiously she couldn't make out a word they said.

The receptionist rushed around the desk. "Volunteering?" he asked, and she nodded without thinking. "Third door down the hall." Then he was gone, along with two other staff members, to stop the escalating fight.

Lisa started to follow them and had to stop herself. The instinct to help wasn't something she could easily ignore.

But she had no business getting involved. When one of the men shoved the other, one of the nurses whistled so loudly, it could have been heard in Brooklyn. The electric danger in the air mellowed.

She sighed as she did an about-face. Why couldn't she get it through her thick skull that she wasn't a cop anymore? Her job now was to be invisible. Minor altercations probably happened all the time in a place like this. They were handling the situation just fine.

The receptionist had mistaken her for a volunteer, which was perfect. Something she should've thought of herself.

She hurried down the long green hallway, saw two doors and entered the one that was open. It looked more like an exam room than an office, but there were three tall filing cabinets in the back, so they probably talked to potential volunteers in whatever room was free. On the wall, there were posters about common STDs, patients' rights and a battered women's shelter.

After checking the open doorway, she walked over to the old metal cabinets. The labels indicated that two of them held legal documents, while the third contained personnel files. Of course it was locked. That wasn't a hindrance, though. It wouldn't take more than thirty seconds to get it open, but it would be a reckless move that could get her thrown out on her ear.

Oh, what the hell. She made sure no one was coming, closed the door and rushed to the cabinet.

She had the right tool in her purse. Bless her brother's training. He could break into anything in any office, and now she was pretty good at it herself. While it wasn't a tactic she was entirely comfortable using, she would know a lot more about Dr. Cassidy after a quick peek at his file.

Before she'd even finished the thought, the cabinet lock popped to the open position. Just as she was about to pull out the drawer, she heard a brief knock. She spun around and pushed the lock in with her shoulder as Dr. Cassidy himself walked into the room.

His gaze was on an open file in his hand, but when he looked up, he seemed surprised. Did she look guilty? She gave him a tentative smile and inched away from the cabinets.

Whoa—howdy—he was good-looking. Even more so than in the picture on the trading card. She was compelled to take a few steps closer, just to confirm that his eyes truly were the color of whiskey. Oh, yes. A well-aged whiskey at that.

He cleared his throat, and she realized she was all up in his personal space. She retreated. Unfortunately, she backed into a cabinet, which then hit the wall behind it with a loud clunk.

Dr. Cassidy didn't seem fazed. He caught her gaze again and with a puzzled frown said, "I'll need you to take off your clothes."

"Wow." Lisa arched her brows. "You guys really take your volunteer screening seriously."

2

DANIEL ALMOST CHOKED on his laugh. He glanced down at the file then back at the gorgeous blonde. "I take it you're not Yolanda."

All she did was smile and he was caught off guard again. It was her lips. They weren't all shiny and covered in goop, just pink and kissable. Not that he had any damn business thinking of her in those terms. She shook her head and her pale hair swept her narrow shoulders, further distracting him.

Damn it, this wasn't like him. Not on the job, patient or not.

"Uh…I assume there's someone who needs an exam, and I'm in the wrong room?" she said.

"That's true." Jesus. Clearly he needed more sleep. "Why don't you follow me and we'll see if we can get this straightened out, Ms….?"

She held out her hand. "Lisa Pine."

"Daniel Cassidy. So, you're here to volunteer?"

"Yes." She let go of his hand. "If you can point me in the right direction…"

"Of course." He led her into the hall when all he should've done was gesture to the adjacent office. "We're supposed to be getting doorplates," he said, wondering when he'd reverted to an awkward teenager. "Are you a medical professional?"

"Nope. Just want to help."

"That's great," he said. "We're perpetually understaffed and overtaxed. A lot of people depend on the free clinics."

"So I've been told."

"Here you are." He opened the door and the woman sitting behind the desk looked up. "Valeria will take care of you," he said and caught the woman's startled expression. Had he gotten her name wrong? No, he was pretty sure that was right. With her side-shaved haircut, the streak of silver in her long black bangs and her numerous tattoos, it wasn't as if he was likely to confuse her with someone else.

"Hello." Lisa moved into the room and glanced over her shoulder the moment his willpower slipped and his gaze landed on her curvy backside. "Thank you, Dr. Cassidy."

He quickly brought his eyes up to her face. "You're welcome. And thank you," he said. "For volunteering."

She smiled.

"Well, I've got patients to see." He backed into the hall and almost took out a passing nurse.

Annoyed and embarrassed, he headed for exam room 4, where his patient had been waiting too long. Before he entered, he gave her file a second look.

According to Yolanda's intake papers, she was a sex worker. A number of them came to the clinic for their health needs. He'd order blood work on her, if she'd let him. Probably not, as all she wanted was antibiotics for chlamydia. "I hope you haven't been waiting too long," he said. "There was a mix-up."

Her disgusted laugh told him he could take his mix-up and put it somewhere uncomfortable. This time, he deserved it.

For the next three hours Daniel barely had time to take a breath between patients. No neurological crises arose, but that was true most days. He was technically here as a specialist, but he'd done a lot of family medicine during his training. Another neurologist, Joseph Glick, usually volunteered twice a month, but he was taking a break for the duration of Daniel's stay.

And Daniel had no idea how long he would be staying. For now, he was content to be there. He liked the freedom and the challenge of this understaffed madhouse. It had no MRIs or CT scanners. Half the equipment didn't work, forcing them to improvise. It certainly kept him on his toes.

Which was probably what bothered his brother about his job. Warren was as concerned about his professional status as he was about his patients. Actually, that wasn't fair. Warren was a great neurosurgeon, in one of the most prestigious practices in New York, and he lived for the work. Daniel had begun to prefer his life to be a little more real, a little less neat.

Like his newest patient, Mr. Kennedy. The old man was snoring up a storm on the table in room 5. Mr. Kennedy squatted in a condemned building a couple of blocks away. He came to Moss Street on a regular basis, sometimes to get a hot drink, sometimes to get some sleep, and mostly because he was a diabetic who didn't take his medication.

It would be a shame to wake him. Which made this a good opportunity for Daniel to grab a quick cup of coffee in what they laughingly called the lounge. Maybe find out more about that new volunteer. His need for caffeine abated as he discovered the woman still in Valeria's office. Filing. "You didn't waste any time jumping into the fray," he said.

Lisa turned at his voice, that smile of hers drawing him inside the office. "Seems they'll take just about anyone."

Valeria's laugh reminded Daniel they weren't alone. "No offense, but that's truer than you know."

"She's signed up for three whole days," Valeria said, and there was nothing feigned about her enthusiasm.

"Excellent. I'm sure she told you about the coffee in the lounge. I was just heading over there."

Lisa blinked and nodded.

He glanced at Valeria, who was watching him closely. The woman was the eyes and ears of the staff. He imagined not much got past her.

"Yes, I did tell her about the lounge, Dr. Cassidy," Valeria said with a hint of amusement. "I even told Lisa where the bathroom was."

Okay, it was past time for him to make an exit. No wonder he rarely dropped by this office. "Can I get you ladies anything on my way back?"

"That's very thoughtful of you." Valeria leaned back in her chair and raised her brows comically high. "I'd love a coffee. Black, no sugar. And if they still have doughnuts, I wouldn't mind one."

He nodded, knowing news of his "visit" would spread through the office like pinkeye. "Black, no sugar," he repeated. "What about you, Ms. Pine?"

"I think it's about time for her break," Valeria said before she turned to Lisa. "Just leave the files where they are. Come back in fifteen?"

When Daniel looked at Lisa, he caught her staring back, a light blush staining her cheeks. For God's sake, he was thirty-four years old and he couldn't have handled this more awkwardly if he'd tried. Talk about showing his hand.

"I could use a cup of coffee." Lisa put down the work and gave Valeria a nod before leading him down the hall.

For the life of him, Daniel couldn't come up with a decent opening line. Though he was content to enjoy the view. Lisa had a nice, easy sway to her walk. Too bad she hadn't worn a skirt. He'd bet she had great legs...

"I understand you're a neurologist," she said with a backward glance. "And that you're single."

"What?" he said, taken aback until he caught the mischievous look in her eyes.

"And you not only graduated from Harvard, but did your residency at Johns Hopkins and just finished a neurology fellowship at Mount Sinai."

He sighed. Gossip was as ubiquitous as penicillin at the clinic. Until today he'd primarily been exempt from it. Or so he'd thought. Nothing he could do about it, though, and in this case, he wasn't sure he minded. "Alarmingly true, but I bet you don't know my blood type."

"O-positive."

He stopped so fast the nurse behind him almost bumped into his back. "Seriously?"

Lisa gave him a wicked grin. "Educated guess. It's the most common blood type."

He pointed his file at her. "You're fixing Valeria's coffee," he said as they entered the lounge. "And even if there are any doughnuts left, she's not getting any."

Her laugh was as charming as her smile, which made the sound of his cell phone ringing in his pocket an unwelcome intruder. What was worse, it was a call from Warren. Even though he let it go to voice mail, his mood plummeted. Of course he knew what his brother wanted. Just as Warren knew Daniel wasn't ready to discuss joining the Center.

He might as well stop thinking about Lisa Pine. Starting something with any woman, let alone a volunteer, was out of the question while his world was in flux. The only thing that mattered to him at the moment was working until he crashed from exhaustion and then repeating the cycle. Filling every nook and cranny of his life with anything that wasn't thoughts of his future. Eventually, he'd have to face his obligations. But not today.

A row of lockers against the wall, the pair of ugly corduroy chairs and two overworked coffeemakers sitting on a folding table allowed for limited space in the small room. It could hold four people nicely; six was pushing it. He reached around Lisa for a cup while watching her carefully study the pitiful selection of leftover doughnuts.

She really was a classic beauty with her flawless complexion, electric blue eyes and blond hair. She wore some makeup, but not much. She didn't play up her looks at all. If anything, she played them down.

She must've felt him staring. Probably regarded him as just another sucker overtaken by her beauty. Hell, her smile alone could make a man do very stupid things. Even a physician who knew a lot about the brain and how it worked.

"I assume Valeria knows these are stale by now," Lisa said, then glanced down and frowned. "Dr. Cassidy? Your phone?"

He still had the cell in his hand. It was his brother again. Daniel didn't have the luxury of turning his cell off, so he might as well deal with this now. "Excuse me," he murmured as he handed her the empty cup.

He was halfway down the hall, planning what he'd text to Warren to make him go away, when it occurred to him he should've said something more to Lisa. It was tempting to go back, apologize for his rudeness. But why bother? Walking away seemed to be what he was best at.

"You came back. I'm impressed."

Lisa nearly ran Dr. Cassidy over when she stepped into the hall on her way to the ladies' room the following morning. The heat rushing to her cheeks was as mortifying as the way she'd dipped her chin until she was looking at him through her lashes. She had no idea where that reaction had come from. The only thing missing was twirling her hair around one finger. "I committed to three days," she said.

"Right. Valeria mentioned that. Another scintillating day of filing?"

She shook her head, very aware of her hair brushing across her shoulders. She'd spent a stupidly long time with her flatiron this morning. "Nope. Screening patients."

"Ah."

Daniel had his lab coat on, but it was open, revealing his dark-colored pants and pale blue oxford shirt. He'd worn a tie, dark blue, and oh… "Are those little pink ribbons?"

He nodded, touching the half-Windsor knot. "Breast-cancer awareness. I have a collection of message ties. They're useful for starting a dialogue with patients. For example, have you done a self-check lately?"

She blushed again. Not because of what he'd said, but because of the image that had popped into her mind. The same image of his hands on her breasts that she'd imagined last night while repositioning her pillow a thousand times.

Their gazes locked. His serious eyes and those slightly parted lips made her mouth go dry while her vaginal muscles tightened. Appalled at the unexpected flare of arousal, she looked away first. This sort of thing—this overwhelming desire to touch and be touched—hadn't happened to her in ages. It wasn't welcome, either.

Daniel cleared his throat as he leaned back, distancing himself without taking a step. "I've got—" He held up the file in his hands. "Maybe I'll see you later in the lounge."

She nodded, unable to think of a thing to say. Although she did release a big sigh when he walked into exam room 1.

She continued on her way, more aware than ever that she'd made a critical error when she'd dressed that morning. Mercifully there wasn't a full-length mirror in the ladies' room. Regardless, Lisa saw her mistake the moment she looked at herself in the mirror above the sink.

Technically, she hadn't needed to return to the clinic, not for the case. Sure, she'd signed up to volunteer for three days but she could have backed out.

In the end, she hadn't been able to resist the allure of Dr. Cassidy. In addition to discovering why he was working at a free clinic, she wanted to know why a phone call had changed his demeanor so drastically yesterday. An emergency she would've understood, but he hadn't even answered it. One second he'd been joking with her and the next, he'd walked away as if she'd ceased to exist. He hadn't even returned for his cup of coffee.

But who was she kidding? The way she'd dressed and the way she'd reacted when they'd spoken made her primary reason for returning embarrassingly obvious. She'd wanted to see him again. She wanted to feel that same jolt of excitement she'd felt yesterday. That yearning for a man's touch she thought she'd smothered for good. For the past year, she'd been very careful, kept to herself, focused only on her new career. The four months before that she'd barely left her apartment. After what she'd been through, she knew better than to get close to anyone, let alone become involved.

But maybe her perspective was too narrow. Sex didn't necessarily mean involvement, right? According to Dr. Cassidy's trading card, he was looking to get married, but before he met his soul mate, she doubted Daniel would object to a night of no-strings sex.

Besides, he wouldn't be with her. Not really. He'd be with Lisa Pine. After two days or even a week, she would disappear and that would be that. It would be like college. She hadn't gone out often, but when she had, she'd made sure there would be no complications. His place only, first names, no sleeping over. The three one-night stands she'd had had been great. Of course that was before she'd met Miles. But she wasn't going to think about him, except as a reminder that she was terrible at picking both friends and lovers.

There was one more hurdle to clear before she could even contemplate sleeping with Daniel: Heather Norris. The odds of her choosing a doctor who worked for free were close to nil. But the fact remained that if Lisa decided she wanted to bed the good doctor, she needed to be damn certain Heather wasn't interested.

Because Lisa sure was. Although sex with him or any man would be a big step for her at this point. One reckless move could have devastating consequences.

She focused once more on her reflection and sighed. No wonder the patients she'd been screening all morning had seemed distrustful. Their vague responses on the intake questions and the way they wouldn't meet her gaze had puzzled her. Until now. It hadn't been because she was a stranger but because she'd dressed to impress Dr. Cassidy, not to blend in.

Rookie mistake. A private investigator was supposed to remain inconspicuous.

The time she'd taken with her makeup should have been a clue. And what the hell had she been thinking, wearing her pale peach silk blouse? She never wore it unless she had somewhere special to go. Helping sick people fill out forms didn't qualify.

Of course she hadn't brought another blouse with her. Or jeans and comfy flats, which would have been appropriate. Luckily, there was a thrift store a few blocks away where she was bound to find another top to wear. A quick glance at her watch told her she had ten minutes to go on

Intrigue Me

her break, but wearing her five-inch heels, she'd never get there and back fast enough.

Instead of worrying when there was nothing to do but wait until lunch, she stopped by the lounge. There were a few doughnuts left, so she fixed a coffee for Valeria as well as for herself and picked up two honey glazed to go.

Valeria's reaction to the impromptu gift was so appreciative it made Lisa squirm. Her motives hadn't been pure, that was for sure. The woman was a font of knowledge when it came to the staff. Maybe Lisa could ask her out to lunch tomorrow.

Very aware of the time, Lisa leaned against the credenza, swallowed a big bite of doughnut and said, "I can't believe I dressed so inappropriately. I don't know what I was thinking."

"You were thinking about Dr. Cassidy," Valeria said. "Can't say I blame you. But don't get your hopes up. You aren't the first girl to try to get something started with him."

Lisa considered pretending to be outraged, but what for? Even if she hadn't come to work wearing silk, Valeria was too sharp to have missed what was going on. "He is puzzling, though. While we were in the lounge yesterday, he got a phone call and he couldn't escape the room quickly enough. I figured it was a medical emergency, but he was wearing a pager, so maybe an ex-wife?"

Valeria shook her head. "Nope, he's never been married," she said as she pushed her chair back far enough to put her heavy black boots up. "I might be wrong. You're different. Dr. Cassidy isn't usually so chatty. He certainly hasn't offered to get me coffee before. Or given a volunteer a tour of the lounge."

"He was just being nice."

"Oh, he's very nice. And very focused on his job. But

he doesn't socialize with the staff." She lowered her voice. "I'm not saying he's a snob, though a doctor like him, you'd half expect him to be."

"You mean because he's a neurologist?"

"Because he's a genius." Valeria looked up at the big round clock above the door and then turned back to face Lisa. "Harvard and Johns Hopkins didn't take him because his family's loaded or even because of his last name. People who know what's what say he's something special. Yet here he is, working late every single night." Valeria shook her head. "As much as we appreciate his help, he shouldn't be here treating STDs and broken bones. It's such a waste. There's got to be a story behind it, but Eve isn't talking, and she's the only one who really knows him."

Lisa took another bite of her doughnut. She'd wondered why everyone called him Dr. Cassidy while they referred to the other doctors as Dr. George and Dr. Carol. The staff obviously regarded Daniel as a cut above. "You said something about his family name. Is he related to Dr. Randall Cassidy, who started the Madison Avenue Neurological Center?"

"Yep. That was his father. He passed several months ago. Daniel's brother, Warren, runs the Center now."

"I'm surprised that— Wow, too many Dr. Cassidys to keep straight." Lisa laughed. "Dr. Daniel doesn't work there?"

"Nope. He came here right after finishing his fancy fellowship. He's been working here almost three months now."

"But he'll probably end up there, right?"

Valeria shrugged. "Probably. But I've been told to keep him on the schedule."

Lisa wondered if there was bad blood between the brothers. Valeria clearly knew more than she'd let on, but the other woman had confirmed a lot. According to Lisa's research, Warren was a celebrated neurosurgeon in his own right, and their father's patients had included Supreme Court justices, senators and leaders of at least three other countries. Lots of big egos to fit in one place. Wouldn't be the first time a family ended up divided by power and wealth.

"You know what?" Valeria put her boots on the floor and Lisa realized her break had ended two minutes ago.

"I say go for it. I think you might be just what Dr. Cassidy needs. Worst thing that could happen is he says no."

Lisa sighed as she pushed off the cabinet she'd been leaning on. "I'm sorry if I've given you the wrong impression." A short consensual fling was one thing, but everyone knowing about it? No, thanks. "Really, I'm not—" She cut herself off when Valeria checked the doorway, a clear sign that Lisa should go back to work. But just as she got to the door, Valeria stopped her.

"I got the right impression. I don't know much about his personal life other than what I've told you. But be careful. Eve makes sure no one gets too inquisitive about Dr. Cassidy and I have no idea why."

"That's the second time you've mentioned her." She'd also heard the name from Mrs. Washington.

"You'll meet her this afternoon. She's been volunteering here for a few years, and she's the one who convinced him to sign up. I don't think she meant him to stay this long, though."

"Huh. Well, he's very nice. And good-looking, but I'm here to work, not flirt."

"I don't know, chica. You seem like a multitasker to me."

Lisa laughed. "You're the one I have to watch out for, you troublemaker." She backed out the door and bumped into a woman in the hallway. "Sorry," she said, taking a half step back as she noticed that the woman's name badge read Eve. "Are you all right?"

Eve gave her a quick head-to-toe assessment and then smiled. "Fine, thanks," she said as she stepped around Lisa and continued on her way.

So that was Daniel's watcher. She was tall, attractive, with dark hair that just hit her shoulders. She was younger than Lisa had imagined. Maybe late thirties. But the air of confidence about her made Lisa curious about her relationship with Daniel.

Whoever she was, Lisa had the feeling Eve would be a formidable foe. Not that a one-night stand was something noteworthy, or wrong, unless Eve was more than just a friend. The last thing Lisa wanted was to get mixed up in a territorial battle. Although Daniel was on a dating-club trading card.

If Lisa had any sense of self-preservation, she'd forget the whole thing. Forget the spark he'd ignited inside her. Feeling numb wasn't that bad. She'd done okay living on autopilot for the past year. Tomorrow, she'd be done with her commitment to the clinic. By the end of the week she wouldn't even remember the color of Dr. Cassidy's eyes.

3

THE ALARM ON Daniel's cell beeped, reminding him that he had to leave in the next five minutes. Eve had asked him to go with her to El Bohio Lechonera, her favorite local lunch spot, and she didn't ask often. He would have loved to avoid it, not because of her company but because of what she wanted to talk about.

He finished up the notes on his last patient—around here, he didn't dare put his paperwork off. Nothing beat a free clinic for sheer volume except for an urban ER.

As he slipped off his lab coat, he thought again about Lisa. He honestly hadn't expected to see her, and he sure as hell hadn't expected to have such a strong physical reaction. Good thing his novelty tie provided a distraction from points south.

It had been a long time since he'd felt this kind of take-no-prisoners want. Plenty of women turned him on, but none of them had kept him awake half the night. Not since high school, at least. Though Lisa hadn't seemed bothered by his abrupt exit from the lounge, he probably ought to give her some sort of explanation. Then ask her out.

Hell, it couldn't hurt to try. He'd wait until she finished her volunteer stint. Simple. It didn't have to mean anything or go anywhere. A night or two would do the trick. Then things could go back to normal.

The distinctive click of heels in the hallway signaled Eve's arrival. She was still on the clock at the Center and most days only came to the clinic the evenings they took appointments. He glanced toward the open doorway and there she was, giving him a very familiar look. The one that said she'd had it up to here.

Too bad. He was fed up, as well. Being his second cousin, Eve had known him since they were kids. She'd been there for him after his mother had run off to France with her art teacher. And he understood Eve had his best interest at heart, but it didn't give her the right to treat him like a disobedient child. Especially given she was only five years older than him. "Would it change anything if I asked you nicely not to bring up my brother or the Center today?"

Eve continued staring at him with nary a blink. "What do you think?"

"Fine." He left the shared office as he'd found it and joined her in the hall. "I'm thinking of letting you pay for lunch."

"Well, don't bother. You keep that brilliant brain of yours busy with the really important stuff. Like explaining for the hundredth time why antibiotics won't help a cold."

He winced, thinking today might be the day they had their little talk. The one where she stopped being so sarcastic about his staying on at the clinic.

"I've got a taxi waiting."

He tapped on the reception desk as they passed, just a quick reminder that he'd be out of the office for an hour. Then he saw Lisa. Her back was to him, but it was enough. Why was he waiting to ask her out? She wasn't his employee. They barely worked together. There was nothing in the Hippocratic oath that said a doctor couldn't date a volunteer. Before he even finished the thought, he and Eve had left the clinic for the warm June afternoon and the waiting Yellow cab.

"New volunteer?" Eve asked as soon as they were on their way.

"Yep. Came on board yesterday and Valeria put her to work filing right away. Today they've got her doing intake screenings."

"Wow, she must be a very good screener for you to know her schedule so well. You didn't say a word to the last recruit I brought in, and she was there an entire week."

"Relax. She's only going to be there one more day."

"I am relaxed. Hey, you're a grown man. You can do whatever you like with whomever you choose."

He didn't hide his frustration when he met her gaze. "Why change now? The last time I had a woman in my life, all you talked about was how it was never going to last."

"I was right."

He grunted, unwilling to continue this game. "You're my cousin, and I love you, but come on, Eve. Knock it off."

"Fine. I won't talk about the fact that she must have a powerful reason to volunteer in the Bronx. Altruism is one thing, but a woman like her? Two months after that article in the *Times* that had your picture on it?"

He shook his head, refusing to be baited. Eve meant well, but sometimes he wasn't sure if she was looking out for him or was jealous. He really hoped it wasn't the latter. "I can't decide between the *Pernil con Mofongo* and the number one combo."

"Get the combo. That way you'll have enough left over for dinner."

"Thanks, Mom."

Eve gave him an eye roll. "Cut it out. I'm in no mood."

"I can see lunch is going to be fun."

"Yes, we're going to talk about you. And Warren. And all the things you wish I wouldn't bring up."

"Yay," he said. "I can't wait."

The taxi pulled over and Daniel paid the driver as Eve went in to try to grab a table. Through some miracle of timing, they had to wait only five minutes for one.

The restaurant smelled like its signature Puerto Rican roast pork, and the casual atmosphere lent itself to loud discussions and laughter. Their orders were taken pronto, and Eve wasted no time getting to the point.

"Warren can't do anything with the house until you remove your things. And that has nothing to do with you starting at the Center. So just bite the bullet and call him."

Daniel held back a sigh. Though he doubted he'd have any luck, he decided to go for one more attempt at forestalling a conversation he wasn't ready for. "You look tired. Out clubbing with the girls again?"

"Thanks a lot, you dick. Two martinis. That's all I had. And yes, I was out with the girls because I haven't done anything remotely fun in over a month. Anyway, I know you're just trying to change the subject, and no, I'm not going there. Warren wants answers, Danny. Is that so hard to understand? You aren't the only one who lost a father."

"Whoa," he said, taken aback. "Going right for the jugular today, huh?"

"This is me, giving you a smack. As much as I love what you're doing for the clinic, you have other obligations. Unless you plan on spending the rest of your life being an unpaid GP in the Bronx."

"Of course I don't. That's not… I'm…damn it, I'm just not ready to leave yet."

She winced. "You made a promise. To take your place at the Center."

"I promised Dad."

"Warren is still your family, and the Center is still your father's legacy."

Daniel flinched and hoped Eve hadn't seen.

"Unless he told you all bets were off when he died?"

He really had to bite down on that one. Their meals arrived, but the churning in his gut made food the last thing he wanted. "Did Dad mention to you any plans for expansion?" he asked, careful to keep his tone casual.

She looked puzzled. "Well, he knew we'd have to hire additional help once you came on board. More support staff, for one thing, and we talked about finding another neurologist. He said once the three Cassidys were there, the waiting list would double. Is that what you mean?"

"Yeah." Just what he'd thought. Eve really didn't know anything about his dad's grandiose plans. She thought Daniel was being stubborn and childish. He wished he could explain to her why he needed more time, but he couldn't. Not until he could figure out what to say to Warren.

It didn't help that he had no idea what his brother was feeling. They were only four years apart, but had completely different temperaments. Warren was more like their dad and the two of them had been really close. Their father had bragged about Daniel, but talked to Warren.

So why hadn't he wanted Warren to know about his very ambitious plans for a whole new approach to their practice? His death had come so suddenly, and so soon after he'd told Daniel about his ideas that Daniel figured he'd died of a stroke. That he'd probably also suffered some mini strokes, and that was why their last and final conversation had been so unsettling. But it was his heart that had given out, and the autopsy had shown no abnormalities in his brain.

The promise he'd made his father wasn't only that he'd work at the Madison Avenue Neurological Center. Discovering his father's true colors had shaken him to the core.

He didn't want to walk into his new life until he completely understood what he wanted his life to be. What the hell was he supposed to tell Warren? Nothing? Should he just pretend the conversation with his father had never happened?

Maybe. But Daniel sure as hell wouldn't forget it. He looked at Eve again. "Dad encouraged me to take some time off after I finished my fellowship."

Eve's mouth opened but it took a few seconds for her to ask, "When?"

"A few days before he died. I'd just finished at Mount Sinai."

"During that private dinner meeting he had with you?"

"Yes." Daniel knew she expected him to elaborate. Wouldn't happen. Eve had been the office manager for sixteen years. She'd started right after graduating from Cornell and no one could have run the busy practice more smoothly. He shouldn't be surprised she'd found out about the dinner. She just didn't know what had been discussed, and it was clear she was hurt by his silence.

"He never mentioned the time off to me," she said, then took a quick sip. "However, I really doubt he meant for you to take three months."

"I'm not ready yet, all right? And for what it's worth, he told me to take whatever time I needed. I wish things were different. But please know I'm not being frivolous. There's a lot at stake here."

"I'm sorry, but I don't understand your hesitation. All you ever wanted was to become a neurologist. To be like him. You don't need to be dealing with stuffy noses and syphilis. You've got a gift, Daniel, and you're wasting your talent."

He exhaled as he shook his head and picked up his fork, although he doubted he'd use it. "You know she's having an affair, right?"

Eve blinked at his non sequitur. "Warren's wife? Yes. And so does he. What difference does that make to your commitment?"

"None. None whatsoever." He took a big enough bite to put an end to the discussion. He knew exactly what he was supposed to do. Help Warren with their father's house, with the trust and the business that was now technically half his. But nothing about that plan was simple anymore.

A minute of silence went by before he pointed his fork at Eve. "Warren stayed home from work for a week after Dad's death. One week. Then it was back to business as usual. He knows I need some time to think things through, but all he cares about is the Center. He could quit tomorrow and have more than enough money to live out his life in luxury. Maybe with his wife, if he even gives a damn about her anymore. But at this rate, with the hours he's keeping, he won't make it past sixty-four, either."

"People mourn in different ways," Eve said, her voice gone soft and sad.

"Exactly. The doctors on staff right now can handle the current patients. I don't care how important they are. The only reason Warren wants me there is because he doesn't think it looks good that I'm working at a free clinic."

"You're not being fair. You know Dr. Elliot planned to retire as soon as you came on board. In view of your dad's passing, he's stayed to help out."

"I think Dad was right. We should consider hiring another neurologist soon."

"Daniel—"

"Look, I know you want what's best for the business and for me. I'm just not sure following in Dad's footsteps is what I want."

Eve couldn't have looked more shocked. She'd worshiped Dr. Randall Cassidy just as Daniel had. But she nodded and gave him a tight smile. "All I'm asking is for you to talk to Warren. Tell him what you've told me."

Daniel shoved aside his plate. "I already have. He just doesn't want to listen."

AT LUNCH, LISA GRABBED a six-inch veggie from Subway on her way to the thrift store. There she found a great blue-and-white-striped sweater and a pair of jeans she liked better than her old favorites. There were shoes for sale, but she drew the line at wearing anything that once held a stranger's foot.

She got back to the clinic with a couple of minutes to spare, so she reapplied her lipstick, stuffed her purse and other clothes in a locker and then checked her phone for messages. She didn't have any, which wasn't unusual these days. After all, she'd cut herself off from virtually everyone who'd been a part of her old life.

Mostly her communications were from Logan or Mike, the investigator who worked with them. Once a week her mom texted. That was, when she and Dad weren't playing in a golf tournament, their latest passion since retiring to South Carolina. Lisa tried to phone them every other Sunday. Their conversations were always brief. They still felt bad about what had happened to her and never knew what to say. Frankly, there was nothing to be said.

As the day progressed, it became clear her change of clothes had paid off. The patient intakes went more smoothly. Sadly, she'd seen Daniel only twice despite staying until six, an hour after they stopped accepting new patients.

She did, however, meet Eve again. Lisa got the impression Eve didn't like her very much. But then, Lisa had only one day left at the clinic, unless she decided to extend her commitment. Which largely depended on what happened with Daniel.

Okay, that made her sound like a lousy excuse for a human being. The clinic needed the help, regardless of her sex life, or lack thereof.

But before she agreed to anything else she'd have to go over the schedule with Valeria. Lisa couldn't let volunteering interfere with her job. It wasn't fair to Logan. And if she wanted to be a truly good person, she'd forget about Daniel altogether. A short steamy fling with him would mean she couldn't return to the clinic as a volunteer.

Not that it appeared as though she'd have to choose. Maybe Eve had said something to him and now he was avoiding her. Dispirited, Lisa went to the lockers and got her purse. When she turned to leave, Daniel was standing just a few feet away.

"Hello again," he said.

"Hi." She paused to dial down the excited pitch of her voice. "You on your way out?"

"I am. Heading to the Upper East Side?"

Damn. "Other direction."

"Ah." He seemed disappointed, which boosted her spirits. "You take the subway?"

"Yep." She wondered why he was standing there and if he even had a locker. Both coffeemakers were off, the carafes rinsed out. The doughnuts were long gone.

"Any chance you…?" His voice trailed off, his gaze drifting past her.

Lisa realized they were no longer alone. The wall with the lockers abutted the exit leading to the back alley. Now that the front door was locked, everyone would have to pass them to leave.

"Excuse me." A nurse she'd met yesterday smiled as she ducked around her.

It took Lisa a moment to realize that she was blocking

access to the lockers. "Sorry," she said and stood closer to Daniel, so close that she was almost pressing into him.

It never occurred to her that he wouldn't move back to give her room. Something that raised the brows of a watchful older woman dressed in pink scrubs.

"You were saying?" Lisa murmured.

Evidently their audience didn't bother him because he was staring at her again, only this time he was up close and personal. She felt his warm breath on her cheek. Felt the heat from his body. The photocopy that she had in her purse didn't do justice to the power of his smile. "I was wondering if—"

"Hey, Dr. Cassidy. You're still here." Hector from the reception desk stood at the doorway.

Daniel sighed and gave his head a small shake of frustration before looking at the man. "Need something?"

Lisa sighed, too. Why couldn't everyone just go away? Couldn't they tell that she was going to say yes to whatever Daniel was asking for? Probably dinner. Maybe more than dinner. But he couldn't ask her with all the interruptions.

"I need a prescription."

"Now?"

"It's for Mr. Kennedy."

Someone bumped into Lisa's shoulder. She stumbled a step and her breast pressed into Daniel's arm. He still didn't move. And she refused to look him in the eye as she straightened. Her cell signaled a text and she was relieved to have someplace else to look.

It was Logan. He wanted the Trading Cards investigation wrapped up pronto. Her breath caught. How could she have forgotten the main reason she was there? Heather hadn't turned down Dr. Cassidy yet, so it was hands-off until Lisa got the word.

She stepped farther back. "I'd better be going."

"Yeah, I've got to…"

Neither of them moved.

"Will I see you tomorrow?" he asked.

Valeria, who wasn't even pretending not to stare at them, had entered the lounge with a student doctor.

"Yes," she said, hating his confused frown. But she couldn't say anything more.

"Good," he said. "Have a nice night."

"You, too."

"Yeah," Valeria whispered as she walked toward the door. "You're here to work, not flirt."

4

LISA ROSE FROM the small table that doubled as a desk and place to eat, mostly takeout since her efficiency apartment had no kitchen to speak of. After making herself a cup of oolong tea, she returned to the laptop and read her report over one last time. While she had several pages of notes, she'd kept the write-up for Heather Norris brief and to the point. Basically, Lisa was giving the client exactly what she'd paid for: an overall picture of Daniel Cassidy, with a focus on his job and an estimate of his income.

Dr. Cassidy appears to be in excellent health. He's a nonsmoker and there's no evidence of addiction. He currently works as a full-time volunteer general practitioner at the Moss Street free clinic, Bronx, NY. His employment began three months ago, and there is no indication that he plans to change his situation in the near future.

Satisfied she'd met her obligation to their client, she hit Send. Just because she knew more about Daniel didn't mean she was cheating Heather. The woman had never asked whether Dr. Cassidy had the ability to turn a woman's knees to Jell-O with only a smile. Or that he had an intensely sexy stare that could result in a serious case of the shivers.

When Lisa hesitated to send a copy to Logan, she was

forced to admit that maybe she'd come close to dipping a toe over the line. Only thing she could really do was move on by investigating Heather's number two pick. Another doctor, this time a dermatologist who had a private practice in Midtown.

She unfolded the photocopy of Dr. Edward Fleming's Hot Guys trading card. Lisa had looked into the dating club for herself. While it seemed completely legit with a slew of satisfied members, Lisa would've done the same thing as Heather and hired a PI to investigate her potential dates first.

Although not for the same reason as Heather. Ms. Norris had made no bones about the importance of the two doctors' earnings. Lisa wanted to know everything she could about a man she'd want to date. Honestly, she didn't really care about their income. She wanted safety. Someone she could trust.

But her own bitter experience had revealed that on a personal level her instincts were horribly flawed. The reminder of what her mistakes had cost had her shifting in her seat. Daniel appeared to meet all of her ideal man requirements, but clearly he had his own issues. There was a reason he wasn't at the Neurological Center.

The last thing he needed was someone like her.

Her sigh sent Dr. Fleming's paper flying off her desk. What a perfect metaphor for the mess she'd made of her life.

She retrieved the photocopy and focused on Edward Fleming. He was looking to date, his favorite restaurant was the Pure Thai Cookhouse in Hell's Kitchen, his passion was flying and according to the woman who submitted his card, he was dependable and sweet.

That was the issue, though, wasn't it? Lisa felt sure all the men on the cards sounded great, but there was no way to tell, really. It wasn't cynicism. She knew firsthand that the people closest to you could turn out to be monsters. Tess had been her best friend, the one Lisa had trusted with all her heart. Tess's uncanny ability to expose liars and cheaters and men with tempers should have raised a red flag, but it hadn't.

She took a deep calming breath. Dwelling on Tess's painful betrayal was counterproductive. More than that, it was damaging. The line between looking squarely at the truth and being sucked into an abyss of self-recrimination was very thin. She'd worked hard to move on, and she wasn't going to blow it now.

Dr. Fleming's name brought up a lot of hits on Google. His eponymous practice came up first. The site was professionally done, with plenty of quick-loading graphics of the before-and-after variety, testimonials and lots of advertisements for all the ways people could look younger. He was a real fan of Botox.

His bio read like a press release, so nothing to go on there. But he used LinkedIn, so...

Her email notification app beeped. Huh. Heather. She was out of town on business and Lisa hadn't expected to hear back so soon. The response was short and to the point: Forget about Cassidy. He's gorgeous, but a bleeding heart. Working for free? No thanks. Let's move on to Dr. Fleming.

Lisa acknowledged the request professionally even though her heart was pounding and the stupid grin on her face felt weird. But she pulled herself together quickly. Daniel was no longer a person of interest as far as McCabe Security and Investigation was concerned, which meant...

No. She wouldn't think about that yet. Heather was still their client, so Lisa went back to work.

Fleming looked more and more like the kind of man

Heather wanted. He golfed. Co-owned a private plane. Belonged to a number of professional organizations and had dozens of connections listed on LinkedIn. In fact, the only mystery about Dr. Fleming was why he wasn't married already.

Once again, she couldn't be sure the information on the trading card was true. For either doctor.

She should call Cory, her friend from her old precinct.

At the thought her chest tightened. Calling him wasn't something to take lightly. He would welcome the contact; she knew that. It was her ego that made the decision difficult.

She went back to work, making notes, clicking on website after website, until it was crystal clear that Dr. Edward Fleming appeared to be a perfect match for Heather. She'd be all over him. Lisa put his trading-card photocopy in her in-box while she pulled out Daniel's.

She stared at his image, only mildly surprised at the butterflies in her tummy. Maybe that was reason enough to never show up at the clinic again. But really, if she kept her wits about her, did a bit more digging, why not have a one-night stand? Especially because she'd already met him. Gotten the scoop on him from his coworkers and patients. Besides, he didn't really know who she was, thank God, because she couldn't ethically set him straight without outing her client.

The moment she typed the final sentence of her report on Dr. Fleming, Lisa surrendered and turned her thoughts to Daniel. Half of her wanted to get that one-night-stand thing going. But the top half still had doubts. There were mysteries about the man. Was it his choice not to work at the Center run by his brother? Or was there a reason he wasn't welcome to practice there? For all she knew, he could have a record. Be an addict. She'd met her fair share of people like him who started with energy drinks then moved on to ADD drugs and worse. Frankly, everything about Daniel made him seem too good to be true.

She really should call Cory.

Leaning back, Lisa went through a whole cycle of deep breathing while giving the matter serious consideration. Calling him was the logical next step. Logan never said a word, but he knew as well as she did that she had a wealth of investigative connections and useful tools at her disposal, and she hadn't used any so far. Her own embarrassment wasn't just crippling her; it impacted the business. With a deep exhalation, she made her decision. It was time to take another step on her road to recovery.

She remembered the phone number. Of course she did. She'd worked at the 36th Precinct for four years. Assuming things hadn't changed too much since her resignation sixteen months ago, she should reach Detective Cory Riley.

"Detective Lisa McCabe." Cory's voice lowered, as if finding it difficult to believe it was really her. Perfectly understandable. She'd avoided everyone from the department for the past year. "Hey, kid, how ya doing?"

Kid. She smiled. While in the academy together, how many times had she reminded him she was a month older than he was. "Ah, you know, same shit, different day," she said, the familiar banter coming more easily than she'd expected even as the reality that nothing was the same, would ever be the same, pressed on her chest like a fifty-pound weight. She wasn't even a detective anymore. Being too trusting had lost her the right to that title. And after having worked so damn hard for it. Trying to make her mark in a good-old-boys network like the NYPD had been a monster of a hill to climb. "How about you?"

"Me? I'm okay. The wife got a kitten. My legs are shredded." He paused and the sounds of the detective's bull pen behind him brought tears to her eyes. "It's been a long time," he said, his voice softer. "God, I'm sorry about what happened. I know I should have called—"

"You did. I got your voice mails. It was me—I wasn't ready…"

"I should've kept calling."

"I just would've reported you for stalking."

Cory laughed. "Yeah, you would," he said, sounding more relaxed. "I can't shake off what happened with Tess. It doesn't seem real. How the hell could she have fooled us for so long?"

Lisa swallowed around the lump in her throat. "You mean me. She fooled me, Cory."

"No," he said after a short pause. "Tess Brouder fooled all of us, even the brass. I keep thinking about our academy days, trying to figure out if there'd been any clues that she was off her fucking rocker. But for the life of me, I can't come up with anything. So, no, kid, you're not alone."

But Lisa was alone in this. It was sweet of Cory to want to soften the truth, but she'd trusted Tess with everything. Including access to all her personal documents.

"They're still trying to figure out how she managed to bypass the precinct's firewalls. Hacking the NYPD took some balls, that's for sure." Cory paused. "You ever get your credit straightened out?"

She didn't want to continue this conversation. The panic attack building inside her wasn't as bad as some, but with her inner voice screaming at her, the weight crushing her chest and now the shakes coming on… Rehashing the most painful betrayal of her life was torturous. No wonder she'd put this off for so long. "It'll take years of rebuilding for me to get back my old credit rating, if I ever can. She really wiped me out."

"Yeah, well, she can't do any more damage now."

Lisa briefly closed her eyes. That wasn't entirely true. Tess's death had robbed Lisa of finding the one thing she was desperate to know: Why? Why go to so much trouble when all she had to do was leave their shared apartment? They weren't even working in the same precinct. And why bother with the other four victims. To try to mask that her primary target was Lisa?

"Cordova's team is still working hard," Cory said. "He knows it was an execution-style hit straight out of the Mafia rule book, but—"

"Nobody's talking." She knew how difficult it could be when a team ran into a roadblock. It would be old-fashioned police work that would net them their next clue, but that could take a hell of a long time.

"He's sure they'll get a break soon," Cory said. "At least you got a copy of that flash drive."

So had everyone else involved with the case. They were all privy to the intimate details of Lisa's life and Tess's utter contempt for her. Lisa hadn't managed to read even half of the filth written about her. "Yeah—" Her damn throat closed up. She cleared it a couple of times. "Anyway, I'm actually calling to ask a favor. You think you could run a quick background check for me? Just, you know, priors, anything that stands out."

"For you? No problem. I'll get right on it and call you back."

"Thanks, Cory. I'll email you the name and address, and if you wouldn't mind emailing me back, I'd appreciate it." Damn it, he had to have heard the wobble in her voice.

"You're missed around here, Lisa. Seriously. Just because that bitch was on some kind of vendetta doesn't mean you weren't a good cop. You didn't ask for any of this."

"I appreciate that." She straightened in her chair. Pushed her trembling fingers through her hair and lied her ass off.

"I'm doing great now as a PI. There's a lot less paperwork, that's for sure. Some of the clients are really interesting."

Cory let out a big sigh and did her the great courtesy of getting off the phone quickly.

Before she did anything else, she emailed him the details. Thank God for spell-check. Once she hit Send, the reality of what she'd just done hit her. She'd guessed it would be bad, rekindling old connections, but that had been like ripping stitches from her tattered soul.

Somehow, she managed to log off the computer and shut it down. Then she got out the Jack Daniel's. She was allowed exactly two fingers. No more. The last thing she needed was to add an addiction to her broken life. She just hoped two fingers would be enough.

DANIEL NEEDED TO do something fast. Working in the clinic while Lisa was in the building wasn't working out so well. Not her fault. She certainly wasn't in his way. But she was a distraction. He had questions. Too many for a woman he'd barely spoken to, and yet they'd kept him up far too late.

He couldn't help wondering if she didn't have to work. Temporarily unemployed? Maybe she worked at home, so coming to the clinic was a way to socialize. If he hadn't interacted with her, he never would've considered she'd find volunteering at a free clinic rewarding. With her beauty and the cool reserve of a socialite, she looked more the fund-raiser type. Like his sister-in-law, for instance, only much prettier. He doubted Warren's wife even knew how to file. But when she smiled and batted her lashes, men pulled out their checkbooks.

Forget being flirty. All Lisa would have to do was walk into the room. But somehow he couldn't see her in that role.

And the staff seemed to like her. He didn't really know the

nurses or clerical personnel, but he overheard them chatting sometimes. They should've hated Lisa on sight. In his experience a woman that beautiful could stir up lots of trouble.

Also, she didn't wear a ring. Or any jewelry, in fact. Just a watch. He hadn't gotten a good look at it, so he had no idea if it was a street-vendor special or something from Tiffany & Co.

Her hair was different today. More casual. Straighter, with longish bangs that brushed her eyelashes. He liked it this way, and he liked that she looked so comfortable in a casual sweater and jeans.

"Dr. Cassidy?"

He blinked. Angie Weeks blinked back, only she was on the examination table wearing a paper gown, while he was holding her open file and daydreaming about Lisa. Yeah, that had to stop.

He quietly cleared his throat. "Anything else I should know about?"

She looked sideways then back, her gaze cautious. "Nope. I figured one STD was plenty."

Right. If he could have kicked his own ass around the block, he would have. "I'll go find out where the nurse is. Then we can finish up quickly. I'll be right back."

"Quickly. Yeah. Sure."

He left exam room 3. Lisa had been on his mind most of the day, but this was the first time he'd let it interfere with an examination. Not just the first time today, but ever. He was meticulous about patient care, and he never took his responsibility lightly. He would be damn sure it wouldn't happen again. Right now, though, he needed a female nurse to sit in on Ms. Weeks's exam. After his patient had been taken care of properly, he would do what he should have done earlier—wait for Lisa to have a break and then ask her to dinner.

IT WAS GETTING RIDICULOUS. After spending all morning
working on the divorce case for Logan, Lisa had looked
forward to coming to the clinic after lunch. But she'd been
pulling files since one o'clock, which had sounded easy
enough until she'd realized these weren't the files in Valeria's office, but in a storage room that smelled of dust with
a hint of mildew. These were old files, patients who hadn't
been seen in six years or longer. The manila folders with
the colored key tabs had been stuffed so tightly into rick-
ety shelves that she hoped all the paper cuts she'd suffered
didn't land her in one of the exam rooms.

Although if it was Dr. Cassidy doing the examining,
she wouldn't mind one little bit.

"Ouch!" Lisa yanked back her hand, muttering a few
cusswords that seemed to help the sting. Once again, the
box of tissues she'd put on the counter came in handy.

Okay, so it wasn't just the tightly packed files turning
her poor fingers into a battlefield that was the problem.
She couldn't stop thinking about Daniel. Not too smart
since her interest in him might've earned her this hellish
job. Apparently her exile was courtesy of Eve.

She shoved another five files into the open box, still de-
bating her next move. Valeria had asked if she would like to
make another commitment to volunteer. Lisa hadn't given
her an answer.

The easy thing would be to say no. That way, Lisa Pine
would disappear into the city, end of story.

The less easy thing would be to agree, but without a
locked-in commitment. She had a full-time job with flex-
ible hours, which was important for more reasons than her
paycheck. Logan depended on her now. Mike, the only
other employee, had transferred some of the office work
to her so he could be of more help with the security side of

the business. But she wouldn't mind coming to the clinic when she had some free time.

Since Tess had stolen her identity and everything else that mattered, Lisa hadn't interacted with many people outside of work assignments. Her choice. She didn't want to make friends. She'd barely wanted to make acquaintances.

But the Moss Street Clinic had made her rethink a few things. Leaving aside the issue of Daniel, she liked working there. It had been only two and a half days, yes, but there was a vibe to the place that let her breathe. It felt safe. Bangers from different gangs could sit in the waiting room without killing each other. Homeless people weren't harassed, and sex workers were treated with respect and courtesy. Everyone was cared for, regardless of past mistakes and bad choices.

So, yeah, she could see making this a part of her life. A few hours here and there.

And then there was Daniel.

Now that Cory's email had given him a thumbs-up, she felt reasonably certain that one night of sex with Daniel would not only be safe, but would cure a lot of what ailed her. It would be a very big step, but she didn't know when she'd have another chance like this. If it worked out, then maybe she'd check into the trading-card thing for herself. But that would be later. Much later. Or maybe never if it made her feel this shaky. What were the odds of her picking the one psycho in the bunch. Pretty damn high.

Besides, she was too busy fantasizing about Daniel Cassidy to even think about strangers on cards.

The question now wasn't whether to sleep with Daniel one time. But whether she could have both a single night of down and dirty sex and a semi-regular gig at the clinic.

She could imagine volunteering as a form of long-term therapy. The clinic was an ideal place to learn how to function now that she had her new armor in place. The idea of actually helping people instead of finding evidence of adultery or embezzlement or tracking down deadbeat dads would help her feel more productive.

Having sex with Daniel would be the first step to embracing her new definition of *intimacy*. Feeling pleasure? Fine. Getting sweaty and wearing herself out? Fantastic. Letting herself trust or feel or care? Never again.

After a heartfelt sigh, another five files went into the box. Then another five.

Even though her shift was over, she kept on working. There were still patients out there, and she hadn't managed a moment alone with Daniel.

A few minutes later he showed up and nearly got himself a knee to the groin. She let out a breath and shifted to give him room. "You scared me."

"Sorry. Wasn't sure you'd be here." He looked good. Tired, but good. "In fact, what are you still doing here?"

"I wanted to finish the row of files I was working on."

His smile increased her already rapid heartbeat. "Don't you know they multiply the moment you turn your back?"

He'd taken off his lab coat, leaving him in jeans and a blue shirt. When he leaned back against the table where the finished boxes went, she moved closer to identify the weird marks on his tie. Viruses, maybe? Bacteria?

"You getting hazard duty pay for this?"

"What?" She looked up, then at the stacks of files still left to do. "Oh, right, I really should, huh?"

"How did you end up with this job?"

Lisa shrugged. "Somebody has to do it," she said and jerked with a start when he touched her cheek.

"Dust," he said, holding up the smudged pad of his thumb as proof.

"Oh, yeah, I'm sure I've got dust in all kinds of places."

Daniel's look of amusement faded as his gaze lowered to her hands. "Jesus." He caught her wrist and inspected her fingers.

Self-conscious, she drew back and pulled out the tissue she'd been using. "They're only paper cuts," she murmured.

"You should be wearing nitrile gloves. That's one thing we've got plenty of in the clinic."

"I hadn't thought of it but you're right." She stared down at her hands and then at his, stunned at how much she wanted him to touch her again. Her cheek, her fingers, she didn't care—she just wanted to feel his warm skin against hers. It had been so long.

She cleared her throat.

Searching her face, he gave her a gentle smile. "May I?"

Wadding up the tissue, Lisa stared down at his extended palm. She laid her hand on his much larger one and didn't even blink when he cupped her elbow and drew her closer.

His hands were solid, comforting and everything she needed. He studied her fingers, but his other hand moved from her elbow to her back. When he stood, they were close enough to kiss.

Looking at him, she could see her own hunger in his gaze. He'd started breathing faster, which made her pulse race.

"I've thought about you all day."

"That's…nice," she said, wondering whether she was supposed to make the first move. Or if him pulling her almost against his body was the first move, and now she was supposed to react.

"And last night."

"Oh," she said, understanding perfectly. "I hope I didn't keep you up late."

He inched forward. There was no longer any shred of

doubt that he wasn't just inspecting her paper cuts. This was it. Her big chance. With a man she'd wanted from the moment she'd seen his picture. One night of down and...

She took a step back as panic ripped through her.

5

DANIEL HAD FELT her tense several seconds before she backed up. Something had changed. She seemed...frightened. He got the feeling that with one wrong move, she'd bolt. At least, after his own step back, he could look at her hand properly. A scar near her thumb caught his attention. It must have happened a few years ago, definitely not more than ten. Someone had done a bad stitching job. The mark could have been barely visible with just a bit more care.

Lisa sighed, and Daniel noticed he was petting the scar with his thumb as if he could fix it. "No more filing for you," he said. "Doctor's orders." He relaxed a little when he saw her smile.

"I'll be sure to tell Valeria you said so." She drew her hand back, but before she turned away, she rubbed her scar.

"Valeria sent you back here?"

Lisa nodded. "Apparently Eve left her a note."

Of course word had spread about the lounge incident. That was inevitable. But Daniel would have a talk with Eve. Find out what the hell she was thinking. Now, though, he took the box from Lisa and stacked it on the others. "So, this is it? Your last day?"

"I'm not sure," she said, wiping her hands on another

tissue and then looking around the room as if she'd forgotten something. "Valeria asked me to come back."

He was of two minds about her returning to the clinic. It would be a lot easier to ask her out if she was finished, but the clinic needed all the help it could get. "I'd say no, if they're just going to stick you back here."

"If everyone did that, the files would never get done."

He shrugged. "You're right. It's late. I'm hungry."

"Oh?"

"Are you?"

The look she gave him made his heart beat faster. Her eyes lit up with pleasure, and he was certain she was going to say yes. But the joy vanished as quickly as it had appeared. "I'm not…" Her sudden interest in his tie sent his hopes plummeting. "Avian flu viruses?" she asked with a laugh.

He glanced down. "Hey, this one's my favorite."

"I have to admit, you didn't strike me as the novelty-tie type."

"Eve bought me a couple the first week I started here. I thought she'd lost her mind. Then I had three more made."

"I think they're great." She checked her watch. "Wow, I have to get moving. Grand Concourse gets crowded this time of day."

"That's right. You live on the Lower East Side?"

She shook her head. "Close, but not quite. Bed-Stuy."

"You know, we could get some dinner. If you wanted. Just dinner."

She sighed, looked at the floor. "Maybe next time."

"Fair enough," he said, keeping things light. "Would you mind some company to the subway?"

"No, not at all. I'd like that."

Her response seemed earnest. He was glad he hadn't pushed. Soon enough they were headed down Moss Street.

It was still light out, which was a pity. Everything was more romantic at night. "I've been curious," he said, as he let the bustle of the city settle around them.

"About?"

He slowed his pace to match Lisa's. "I know you came in at one today. Yesterday, you were here in the morning."

"Are you asking if I work?" she asked. "I have a job, but I do it mostly from home. I choose my own hours."

"What do you do?"

"I work for my brother's company. He does security and investigations. I do a lot of paperwork."

They passed a bar that was notorious for blaring hip-hop from their rooftop. The ongoing battle between the police and the owners had started in the '70s and never quieted down. "Sounds interesting," he yelled.

She laughed and waited until Lil Wayne faded to a bearable level. "Paperwork is rarely interesting."

"Then you come to the clinic and get asked to do filing. That has to suck."

She looked as if she was holding back a laugh. "I like helping out."

He wanted to make her smile all night.

"To tell you the honest truth," she said, "I'm about as boring as they come."

"Somehow I doubt that. When do you catch your train?"

"In twenty minutes."

He'd hoped for more time with her. "We could share a cab."

"We live in opposite directions, remember?"

He opened his mouth to lie about forgetting something he had to do in Bedford-Stuyvesant, but Daniel couldn't even recall when he'd last been to that part of Brooklyn.

They walked a little more slowly and a little closer together. At just past seven, there were a lot of people around, but not half as many as there would be in another hour or so. All the guys eyed Lisa, but she ignored them. Otherwise, no one paid them much attention as they passed a bodega, a pawnshop, Blimpie, a tattoo parlor and another bar. This one kept the music mostly inside.

"Have you always lived in New York?" He pushed his left hand into his pocket to stop from touching her.

She met his gaze again. Their steps slowed to a crawl, but she didn't seem to mind. "Born and raised in Brooklyn. What about you?"

"Also a native," he said. "Upper East Side."

"Did you always want to be a doctor?"

"Yeah," he said, and then someone bumped his shoulder. Daniel angled himself in front of Lisa, but the man kept walking, cursing him in Spanish. Easing back to her side, he didn't settle into his stride again until their shoulders brushed. "My father was a doctor. I used to go to his practice when I was a kid. I liked looking at all the books and the big anatomy pictures on the walls. Come to think of it, I was pretty creepy. Destined to end up as a doctor or a zombie hunter."

"I think doctors earn more than zombie hunters, so I'd say you made a great choice."

"Yeah, but I would have had an awesome business card."

She completely stopped before she looked at him this time, her eyes so bright with amusement, he changed his tune about the night. He'd never have seen the gold flecks in her irises if he hadn't walked with her in sunlight. The moment stretched and neither of them blinked.

After a quick nod, she said, "Go for it. Not too late to switch careers, right?"

Surprised, he laughed. "This from the woman who thinks she's boring?"

"Or you could just have the cards made up. Pass them around at parties."

"That would make me a head case, not a neurologist. But I can see how people might get confused."

"Best to keep them guessing, don't you think?" A tiny twitch at the corner of her mouth ruined her attempt at a straight face.

So did the mischief in her eyes. He could stare into them for hours. That blue. Was it cerulean? What the hell? He had no idea what cerulean looked like. All he knew was that they were beautiful, just like the rest of her. Damn it, he wanted her. Screw the clinic, he hoped she decided not to come back so he could take her to every great place in Manhattan. Right now, he'd settle for touching her hair. Letting it sift through his fingers. A prelude to the moment it brushed against his bare chest.

"Come on, keep it moving. You're blocking the damn sidewalk." A bodybuilder nudged Daniel's shoulder as he pushed his way in front of them.

Daniel tried to recapture the moment, but the idiot had blown it. Lisa walked faster, which wasn't a tragedy in itself, but still.

They rounded the corner, and he could already smell the food carts near the subway. He wished they'd gone to dinner. Somewhere they could share a good bottle of wine. Followed by great sex at her place. "You know…if I got us a cab…"

Her step hesitated, her eyes lowered. Shit. His own misstep was worse. "Thought not," he said, "but the night feels too good to just go home."

She nodded, walking again at his side.

While his attempt at getting her on a real date had ended ignominiously, the play would go on. There were too many looks between them not to try again. If she decided to come back to the clinic. Or she offered her phone number.

"Actually," she said finally, "I still have work to do for my real job."

"Ah. Right." It occurred to him she might be meeting a boyfriend. Maybe she even lived with a guy. He hoped not. "When will you decide about coming back to the clinic?"

"I'll call Valeria tomorrow morning."

That told him nothing.

She glanced at her watch again, and this time she really sped up. He should have paid more attention to the clock. When they reached the top of the steps, he spotted an empty cab stopped at the light. They looked back at each other and their gazes locked again. Two seconds later, he leaned down while she tipped her chin up.

He kissed her. Hadn't planned to. Thankfully, she kissed him back. Pulling her closer caused the kiss to deepen. The feel of her against him tested his self-control. He kind of liked the way they met along the high points. The very tips of her breasts, her right hip, his right knee.

He wanted to part his lips and hope for the best, but he didn't. She was in charge. When she touched his arm and brushed her lips across his, the tip of her tongue followed the same path. He hoped she would leave her lips parted, but instead she stopped the kiss, but didn't step away from his arms.

God, she smelled fantastic, even after being in that horrid room. He honestly hadn't realized how petite she was until they were this close. Of course, that wouldn't matter when they were both horizontal.

"I have to go," she said, turning toward the stairs. She took the first step then she paused. "I'll come in tomorrow afternoon. If Valeria needs me."

"I'm pretty sure she will."

She tilted her chin down. "My train."

He tilted his to the left. "My taxi."

She laughed. It was the best.

LISA MISSED HER STOP. She got out at Nostrand and caught the C going south. She didn't mind. She hadn't lied about the work waiting for her at home, but all she wanted to do was remember that kiss. Not just the kiss, which was far too rushed and too public, but the man who let her set the pace.

It had been perfect. A soft reentry to the world of dating. He'd wanted to deepen the kiss, hold her tighter. His body had thrummed with energy and desire. For *her*.

She hadn't even meant to turn him down for dinner, but she'd gotten scared. God, she was like a stalking survivor or something. What did you call it when someone stole your identity and the rest of your world? *Identity theft* didn't cover it.

Unwilling to go to the dark place when she wanted to ride the pheromone train all the way till morning, she touched her lips. Remembered. God, she'd tasted him. Just a little, but enough to know she wanted more. If she did her work superfast, she could go to bed early. She wouldn't even need her vibrator.

DANIEL HAD JUST finished going over a patient's chart and was about to enter room 3 when a woman's scream stopped him cold. It had come from the waiting area and was followed by more shouting and children crying. Staff and patients were sticking their heads out of exam rooms as he ran down the hall to the front. The real fear hit when he saw the unflappable Hector frozen behind the reception desk.

That was all Daniel could see but he heard the mounting hysteria, then felt a hand on his shoulder and turned to see that it was one of the nursing students. She looked terrified and could barely croak out, "He's got a gun."

"Have the police been called?"

Eyes wide, she seemed confused. "I think so."

"Make sure they have." He glanced over her head at Valeria, who looked equally frightened. "Stay back. I'm just going to check out the situation."

Walking slowly and calmly, he put down the chart in his hand. Then he rounded the corner. A man he didn't recognize was waving a gun. He was short and whippet-thin. The room was crowded with adults sitting in the plastic chairs and wide-eyed kids staring from the play area in the corner.

"Sit your ass down," the guy said when a young woman tried to reach her crying child. "Or I'll shoot you both."

With a choked sob the distraught mother sank back in her seat.

Hands up, Daniel walked into the main room, ignoring Hector and everyone else. All he could see was that the gunman was high on something. Likely meth. From the look of him—torn Kanye T-shirt, filthy jeans, huge pupils—Daniel figured he was tweaking now, when he was least stable.

"Who the fuck are you?"

It was everything Daniel could do not to duck when the bastard waved his weapon at him. "I'm a doctor. If you tell me what you want, I'll make sure you get it. No one needs to get hurt."

"I already told you Nancy's in there. She stole my shit. That's what I want. You've got two minutes to get my shit, or people are gonna die. You got that?"

He waved the gun so wildly, Daniel was afraid it would

go off any second. But he needed to stall until the police came. "Is Nancy a patient here?"

"What the fuck do you think? She ain't no doctor. The lying bitch."

Out of the corner of his eye, he saw Hector carefully getting the people closest to him to duck low and run around the corner to the hallway. But it was the little ones who had Daniel worried. They were too far away from Hector. Where were the goddamn cops?

"Okay," he said, taking one step closer to the junkie. He could crash anytime, or worse, stay tweaked. "I'll go back and get her and your stuff. As soon as you let the children go."

The weapon stilled for the longest moment, pointed straight at him. Shoving back his greasy blond hair, the guy's unfocused gaze shifted to Daryl, Alexis Washington's nine-year-old grandson. "I ain't letting anybody go," he said and grabbed the boy's collar. "I'm gonna shoot you first. Then I'm shooting this kid. How you like that, Doc?"

Mrs. Washington let out a screech and lurched off her seat. The women on either side of her caught her arms. But she screamed at the junkie to let her baby go. He swung the gun toward her.

"Hey," Daniel said, hoping someone could shut her up. "Look at me. I'm the one who can help you." Holding his hands up higher, hoping the idiot's eyes would track them, Daniel lost what he was going to say when the front door opened and Lisa walked in.

He wanted to shout for her to run, but they'd finally quieted Mrs. Washington. The calmer the junkie stayed, the better off for everyone. Including Lisa. Jesus. Why now? Why hadn't she seen the gun through the window and turned around? Daniel couldn't let himself be distracted by her.

She dropped her purse. Loudly. "What's going on?"

The gunman did a 180, pulling a crying Daryl along with him.

Daniel rushed forward, but came to a halt when Lisa held up her hands like stop signs instead of surrender. If that prick hurt one hair on her head, Daniel would tear him apart like only a doctor could.

"Get over there, Barbie." The gun waved, wobbly again. "'Fore I mess up your pretty white shirt."

Daryl cried louder.

Lisa kept walking. Her eyes were wide, her hands in clear sight. "Use me," she said, in the gentlest voice. "Take me instead of the boy, okay? I'll be good. I'll be so good. I'll do just what you want."

Daniel's heart nearly burst out of his chest. He couldn't see the gun from where he was standing. Jumping the son of a bitch was out of the question.

He was on the brink of coughing to call attention to himself when Daryl ran as fast as he could toward his grandma. When Daniel looked back at the junkie, Lisa was so close to him, Daniel couldn't see what she was doing. Jesus, he had no way to tell where the gun was. He had to find a way to get Lisa and everyone else to safety. Now.

Just as he took a step closer, praying he wouldn't get Lisa killed, he heard a loud grunt and suddenly the gun was skittering across the floor and the junkie hit his knees. Daniel froze when Lisa stopped the man's fall. Thin as he was, the guy still outweighed her by a good forty pounds, but she twisted his arm up behind his back and pushed him to the floor. On his way down he briefly met Daniel's gaze, looking like a man who'd just gotten spanked *hard* by Barbie, and she hadn't broken a sweat.

Another grunt came when his hands were yanked together and Lisa planted a knee on his back. "Daniel, can you get the gun? Did anyone call the police?"

He just stood there. He still wasn't sure what had happened, only that it had happened in less than a minute.

"Daniel?"

He nodded, picked up the gun.

"I'll take it if you don't mind."

As if he would disobey her now. He gave her the gun, then moved back when she told him to. With one hand on the prostrate junkie's neck, she did something with the gun that made the magazine fall out.

She was a hell of a lot more at ease than when he'd checked out her paper cuts. One thing was for certain: she hadn't learned those moves pushing paper for her brother's security and investigations firm. Or perhaps she'd had a more personal reason to learn self-defense.

His musing was interrupted by two screaming cop cars parking right in front of the building, and more immediately by Mrs. Washington, who marched up to Lisa and the junkie, then whacked the guy in the head with her purse.

"Don't you go messin' with my baby."

He only groaned. Whether his body was ready for it or not, he was now in the crash stage of meth addiction, which wasn't a place anyone wanted to be, let alone for a long time.

"How'd you do that?" Mrs. Washington stared at Lisa with curiosity and awe. "You some secret agent?"

Lisa shook her head, but couldn't explain because the police were now inside, trying to figure out what had happened and how the tiny blonde had ended up on top.

As Daniel made sure the nurses and med students were taking care of the witnesses, he kept stealing glances at Lisa. The way she was talking to the cops made them relax.

Nod a lot. She'd already proved she had everything under control.

The minute she turned from the cops, she pointed at Mrs. Washington but spoke to the group at large. "Every one of you needs to learn self-defense. No excuses. You hear me? You never know what you're going to walk into. Or what's going to fall on your head. Protect yourselves."

Lisa walked past Daniel, giving him the slightest dip of her head. He followed her, and it was interesting how the folks still in the hallway parted to clear the path. It wasn't hard imagining her in one of those skintight superhero costumes. She sure had the skills for it.

When she got all the way back to exam room 4, she walked in the open door.

He followed her right in, turning the lock behind him.

6

LISA PRESSED HER lips together as she stared at Daniel. Adrenaline screamed through her body and it was all she could do to be still. She wanted him. Now. When this hot-white heat burned away everything she'd been afraid of and every inhibition.

"You were…" Daniel took a step away from the door. "I have no idea how you got that bastard to his knees but, God, it was—amazing."

Her arms were bent at the elbow and her tightly fisted hands rested against her clavicle. She shook them out, trying to temper the fire inside. "I know." She was panting now. Why was he by the door? She wasn't going anywhere.

"You've done this thing a lot, then?" he asked, but there was no hiding his dilated pupils, the way his nostrils flared.

"Not for a long time."

"It must feel—"

"Amazing. I was on fire."

His breathing had accelerated, lifting his chest higher and faster. Those black eyes were a warning. A promise? God, she hoped so.

Daniel moved closer. "How long does this part last?"

She shook her head, barely blinking, watching, watching everything. "Don't know. Twenty minutes, maybe?"

"That's not too long. The drop will be epic."

"Depends."

"On?" He took another step.

"What I do to expend my energy."

His smile was cautious. "Anything I can do to help?"

"There is. But it'll be risky."

"Really?"

She didn't answer in words, just gave him a very louche shrug. Which was an effort, considering she could probably run all the way to Brooklyn. "You do realize I'm not going to be able to keep this up. I'm wound tighter than a Swiss watch, and something's gonna give."

"Can I do something real quick first?"

"Like what?"

"Take your pulse? Make sure you aren't hurting yourself?"

She didn't uncurl her fists yet. "Yes, you may. And it would be extra nice if you could fill me in about what happened before I arrived at the scene. You were going for him, weren't you?"

He picked up a blood pressure cuff. Shaking his head, he said, "That's some disguise you wear. It fools everyone, doesn't it?"

"Not everyone." She could barely stay still long enough for him to check her out.

He finished, tossed the cuff on the exam table, then pulled her into his arms. "You were magnificent," he whispered. "Like a superhero."

"More like someone who knows her strengths." She relaxed just enough to hug him back. "I have a feeling you were pretty super yourself. I mean, you were right there, in range."

"I was just stalling until the police came. But you got here first."

She laughed. "Beats filing."

He laughed with her, and his eyes grew darker. The way he held her was a bit sideways so she only felt his thigh. As if she didn't know he was as turned on as she was. When he sniffed her hair, she pressed into him.

"You smell like honey."

"I don't. My shampoo does."

"Well, I like it. Damn," he murmured when she moved her thigh. "You're a very distracting woman."

That smile of his. It was wonderful. And so was the hand that rubbed her back. If she got on her tiptoes, and he met her halfway, she could kiss him.

He read her perfectly and lowered his head. The kiss was glorious. A stroke of his tongue at the front of her upper palate, a nip on her bottom lip. Then he pressed against her as he thrust into her mouth, their rhythm perfectly in sync, possessive, unguarded and hot as hell.

She moaned when he brought his hand between them and cupped her breast.

"Shh," he whispered. "Don't make a sound."

Okay, this was getting even more interesting. Silence wasn't big on the list of things she was good at. Not during sex. "I don't know if I can."

"You can do anything," he said, and how was he already unzipping her slacks?

She grinned. "So it's going to be fast, quiet, with dirty tricks thrown in?"

"We keep condoms in all the exam rooms. But that means moving next to the sink."

She was so wired, she could probably start electrical fires. They were marching toward danger, which made her want him all the more. The door might be locked, but that didn't mean they wouldn't be discovered. Public sex wasn't her thing, but this? Her breathlessness was a sure sign that she was up for the challenge.

He kissed her again, then literally danced her around until they stopped at the sink. When they had to take a breath, he held up a red packet in triumph.

"Bravo. I guess we each have our secret skills. I didn't peg you for a dancer."

He dipped her so quickly she gasped, then grinned. "Why not?" he said, his lips just shy of hers. "Dancing is a lot like making love."

"Not the way I do it."

They both laughed, his deep and sexy, hers a quiet giggle. Then she was standing again, right by the exam bed.

He was quicker than she was. He'd opened the top button of her pants, and he was starting to push them down her hips.

She couldn't reach between them yet. But once her behind felt nothing but air, she made her move. He put his big hands on what he'd uncovered, then gave each cheek a squeeze she'd remember for a while.

It was time for him to drop 'em, and when she saw an opening, she took it. She slipped straight down into a crouch, eye level with the prominent bulge in his finely tailored trousers. All things being equal, she gave him a little squeeze back, enjoying the muffled moan only she could hear.

Quickly she had his belt open, button undone and zipper down. She stood up again. "The rest is up to you, Dr. Cassidy."

He took her mouth in a savage kiss, and that was the end of chatting. They'd spent too much time in the room already, so he'd have to move fast. She had a feeling a quick rub in the right place would send her right over.

He got off to a good start by lifting her up until she sat at the edge of the exam bed from the side. Her butt made the paper beneath her crackle. When he released his cock from those snug boxer briefs she got to see his pre-orgasmic bliss face. A moment and a quiet hiss later, he ripped open the condom, and then his hands disappeared once again.

She loved that he still had his lab coat on. If only he'd been wearing his stethoscope, she could have stored enough doctor fantasies for years to come.

A cocky grin told her he was ready, and a surprise finger inside her told him her condition in return. He didn't waste another second.

When he entered her, she'd been prepared for hard and fast, but what she got was hard and achingly slow. Enough for her to want to kick off the pants that dangled from her left ankle so she could kick him into gear. He had to know that she was in no mood for slow, but it clearly didn't matter.

"Come on!"

"Shh," he whispered. "We'll get there. I promise."

"When? Next year? Hurry. Before someone comes."

His eyes narrowed. "I've been watching the clock since I locked the door," he said, his whisper a lot more controlled than her own. "I know precisely how long we've been in here."

He pushed into her and in her attempt to be quiet she'd bitten her lower lip so hard it was amazing it didn't bleed. Besides, she was distracted from the pain by the way Daniel was revving up, making her work for it.

He thrust again, harder. Another, one nearly lifting her from the crinkly paper she was destroying. Holy hell, three in a row.

"What are you doing?"

"You can still speak? I need to take it up a notch."

She moaned into his chest, liking his smell. She doubted

it was his body wash, either. It was too real for that. No, it was the man she was smelling. Big, strong— "Oh, God."

One slow, four fast and now his thumb was on her clit. She pretty much stopped breathing because—his thumb. It was— Oh, God. She was resting most of her weight on one hand, the other was on his back, and the way he was hissing reminded her to keep her nails to herself.

The only way she managed to stay quiet as she was masterfully taken apart was by smashing her face harder against his chest. But this time, she licked him. Bit him. Not hard. Well, not too hard.

He was going to bruise like crazy tomorrow. But that didn't stop him. He kept working her clit, his thrusts coming at a punishing pace, and she was on her way to a spectacular orgasm.

"Oh, Christ, I'm going to come," he said, his voice wrecked and sexy as hell.

"Me, too," she mumbled before she let her head loll back. "Right there, right there, God, mphhh…"

He came as she was still jerking around like a badly strung marionette.

At least she was only panting now. Panting as if she'd just run ten miles.

"You okay?" he asked, his breathing as deep as her own.

"Great. Now I have to learn to walk again."

"Can't help you there. I'm barely able to take care of… things."

"You're a good man, Daniel. Thanks for that. What's our time?"

"Twenty-two minutes." He pulled out and then made sure she was sitting far enough back that he could bend over and rescue the lower garments still dangling off her left foot. On his way, he nipped her inner thigh, and she might have blown the whole deal by squealing.

It wasn't easy, but she managed to dress while he washed up. She wasn't about to ask what he was going to do with the condom. Frankly, she didn't give a damn. She was swimming in endorphins and euphoria.

"Can you stop grinning like the Cheshire cat for a moment and tell me if I look like a professional physician?"

She cleared her throat. "You look very good. For a day when you were almost shot."

"You, I'm sorry to say, do not. But you can stay a little longer in the room. You might want to check your hair. Maybe stop smiling so hard?"

"Fine. I'll make myself presentable, but I don't see why I can't be happy for the rest of the day. I mean, I did just take out a gun-wielding maniac without a single shot being fired."

His smile was much softer than it had been earlier. This one was safer, closer to the one he used for patients. "You're right. Smile all you want. Besides, as soon as you're done in here, I'm shipping you home."

"What, you're embarrassed about me already?"

"No." He sounded highly insulted. "For God's sake, I am a real doctor, and you've been through a traumatic event. You need to go home. Take it easy. Maybe you have a therapist…?" He paused to study her and she wondered if he thought she'd learned the defense moves because she'd been victimized. But no, then sex would've been off the table. "This isn't something to treat lightly, despite, well…" He waved between them.

"I don't need therapy, thank you. And I don't know about going home." The adrenaline ride had reached its peak. "I'm fine."

She could see exactly how much he disagreed with her plan. "I'm calling a cab for you. No arguments."

"Oh, all right. Although I'll have nothing to do at home except work."

"Improvise."

She hopped off the table, fixed her clothing then went to the mirror. Behind her, Daniel was tidying up. She looked ravished. "Oh, my God."

"What?" He was at her side in seconds.

"We had sex."

"I know."

"No, you don't… It's just…"

"Are you sorry?"

"Not at all. Surprised. But I guess that's appropriate. Although, I had sort of thought we'd start by meeting for coffee?"

He kissed the side of her head and smiled. "I think we can still manage that."

Now that she was getting back to normal she'd have to think about it. God, she'd actually had sex with him. She finger combed her hair, but it still looked pretty crappy. "You might consider a therapist."

He reared back. "Are you serious?"

"You've been through a traumatic experience yourself." She turned to him, pulled him close by his lab-coat pockets. "My advantage is that I've been trained in martial arts. I know how to calm myself. No one got hurt, so that's another plus, but I'm guessing you haven't been faced with something like this before."

"Uh, medical emergencies?"

"Not the same. Your life was at risk. It's a big deal. Don't play it down. Having expertise in one area doesn't mean you can ignore a trauma. I'm sure if you diagnosed you, you'd agree."

"Yet you don't need a therapist," he said, looking entirely too curious.

"I have someone if I need to talk." She went on tiptoe to kiss him. She couldn't deal with questions about herself, not now. Maybe never. "Now, I need to leave this room, and so do you. We should walk out as if we hadn't…"

"Right. Together. But check again. Do I have your lipstick on me?"

She looked, tempted to kiss him again. "Nope. Do I look appropriate for the circumstance?"

"Yes. Does it smell like sex in here?"

She winced. He bent at the sink, pulled out a fragrance-free air cleaner, which actually did have a fragrance, but since it wasn't sperm, it was fine.

"Just, before we go out, please note that I'd like to have that coffee at your earliest convenience."

"Me, too." She sighed and touched his face. "I'll remember this for a long time."

"Me… Okay, now we're looping. Let's head out."

He opened the door for her, and she left the room to find a very appreciative and concerned group of staff and patients in the waiting room. Mrs. Washington was still there, and she was holding Daryl's hand. "You all right?"

Lisa nodded. "I was rocketing with adrenaline and shock, but Dr. Cassidy was right there for me. So, I'm going to go home, and get some rest, but I'm fine. How about you?"

"We're good. Mostly 'cause of you. But there's a pediatric therapist coming here shortly, and she's gonna talk to Daryl."

Lisa crouched in front of the somewhat clingy young man. "You were so, so brave," she said. "I am so proud of what you did. I bet your grandma is, too."

"Granny," he said.

"Right. Good to know. Do you have any questions for me?"

He looked down, then up again, hiding a little behind his granny's arm. "Do you know Spider-Man?"

She put on a thoughtful face and then shook her head sadly. "No, I don't. I wish I did, though. He's a great hero."

Daryl nodded.

"Go on," Mrs. Washington said. "You can tell her. She won't bite."

Daryl dragged his sneaker on the linoleum. "Thank you for saving me. And you is—"

"You are," Granny said, a gentle correction.

"You are real pretty and brave, too."

She held out her hand. "We were both brave today. I think we should shake on it."

He took her hand and pumped it twice, harder than Lisa was expecting. Laughter followed, and that was a very good sign.

When she stood up, Daniel wasn't there, but he came from the back office a few moments later. "I'll walk you out."

"You don't have to," she said. "I'm fine. Thanks. You must have a lot of patients who haven't been seen yet. If I feel shaky, I know who to call."

"Good. I'm glad. I'll speak to you soon?"

"Soon. Yes. Oh, great, where's my purse…?" She glanced around, then felt someone shove it into her hands.

Daniel was still watching her.

God, what the hell had she just done?

7

TWO BLOCKS FROM the clinic, Lisa walked out of the café sipping her go-to comfort drink, a hazelnut double shot latte. It was early, just after nine, and she'd stayed up late last night writing reports so she'd be free to come to the clinic.

Not only to see Daniel, but to find out if Valeria was going to kick her out on her ass. How could she have been so reckless? What on earth had she been thinking, having sex in an exam room? With all those people just outside in the waiting area?

That was the thing—she hadn't been thinking at all. The adrenaline-rush excuse could only go so far. She knew better. That clinic was a hotbed of gossip. And yes, she did care what the folks there thought of her. Then there was Daniel. If he'd been accused of something unethical, and it was her fault? She'd never forgive herself.

But the real kicker? Once she'd finally crawled into bed last night she'd stayed up for hours picturing how Daniel had looked when he'd had her up on that exam table. She should've been drowning in humiliation, not getting hot for him all over again. Anyone could have heard them. Everyone could know.

She should turn around and go back home. Do her job like a regular person. Forget Lisa Pine ever existed.

Unfortunately, she didn't think the ache in her chest had anything to do with the clinic. Daniel Cassidy had been her first step out of the prison she'd created for herself. He'd awakened hope. Courage. A new beginning. Which sounded great, but the fall would be far and crushing if yesterday had been the mistake she feared.

The moment Lisa walked into the clinic she knew right away no one had heard anything. Some might suspect, but she definitely didn't have anything to worry about at the moment. Not when there were a ton of people in the waiting area. Standing. Applauding *her.*

It was humbling and wonderful and it choked her up until she could barely hold back tears.

Waving her hands in an attempt to get everyone to stop was useless. Mrs. Washington was there along with her grandson. In fact, there were a lot of patients she'd seen yesterday afternoon. Ah. She'd left, but it couldn't have been business as usual after all that drama. The only person she didn't see was Daniel.

"Sit down." She had to raise her voice three times. Even so, no one sat, but at least they did stop clapping.

"Where'd you learn to do all that kung-fu stuff?"

Lisa recognized the voice coming from the reception area. It was Melanie, one of the nurses on rotation. "Aren't you supposed to be working? Is anyone seeing patients?"

Melanie laughed. "It's your fault half the folks here didn't get seen yesterday."

"Oh, no." Lisa inched toward the hallway. "Don't lay the blame on me. I was minding my own business—"

"You took that boy down so hard he don't know which end is up anymore."

Lisa slid Mrs. Washington a look. "You got a pretty good whack in there yourself."

The *grand dame* of Moss Street made her way through the crowd. She looked down at Lisa. "Little thing like you, I wouldn't have believed it if I hadn't seen it with my own two eyes. Where'd you get all that fancy footwork from?"

"Self-defense classes. I told you—"

"Hold on 'bout that. First I want to give you somethin'. Daryl?"

Her grandson was right behind her, using both hands to hold a covered plate. She took the dish and handed it to Lisa. "Thank you for protecting my baby. For protecting all of us. This here's my world-famous cracklin' corn bread. Old family recipe I ain't never told a living soul."

"Thank you, Mrs. Washington." Lisa took the plate and almost dropped it, it was so heavy. "I'm glad I was able to help. You were the first person to welcome me to the clinic, and you were so friendly, I went and signed up to volunteer."

Mrs. Washington puffed up even larger than her big hair. "I said Dr. Cassidy was good, didn't I? He knowd how to fix you up just right."

Lisa almost dropped the plate and her purse. If Mrs. Washington knew about what she and Daniel had done in the—

Of course she didn't. Dr. Cassidy had fixed up her *headaches*. Lisa nodded in full agreement, taking tiny steps backward. "He is a very good doctor. You know what? I'm going to go put this corn bread somewhere safe. I'm not sharing this with anyone."

"Smart girl," Mrs. Washington said. "And honey, you can call me Mrs. W. All my friends do."

Lisa really was touched, and she hoped it showed, but she couldn't stand one more second in the spotlight. As she turned to leave, Melanie said, "Come on back and tell us more about that self-defense. I wouldn't be afraid to go down to the bodega at night if I could kick ass like you."

"I promise," Lisa said, hurrying away from the chatter. She would talk to them about self-defense because they needed to know. But she had something equally important to do right now.

Instead of heading into the lounge, she scurried straight back to exam room 4. Just to check if she'd left anything. She didn't think so, but still… It was occupied, but since it shared a wall with the filing room, she went there instead. After putting the dish on the gurney, she pressed her ear to the far wall. Nothing. She couldn't hear a thing. But she wouldn't be satisfied until she'd spoken to Daniel.

She'd moved two banker boxes that she'd left open the day before yesterday when the door swung open behind her. She spun around so fast, she almost lost her balance. "What are you doing here?"

Daniel blinked at her. "Me? What are you doing here? I thought you weren't coming in today."

"Making sure we hadn't left anything incriminating behind and that we weren't going to be tarred and feathered."

"I checked exam room 4 earlier. There's no indication that anyone has an inkling. In fact, they all seem to think I'm nicer now. Everyone is smiling at me."

"Well, someone might get an inkling if you keep coming to the filing room." She couldn't believe he hadn't left immediately. "Go. Now. Before someone catches you."

"I'm going. But we need to talk."

"Fine. Yes. I agree."

"Dinner?" he asked, half a step out of the room.

"No," she said. "Coffee. Now out."

The second he'd closed the door behind him, she wished they'd kissed when they had a chance.

God, she was hopeless.

FOR ONCE, THE waiting room was quiet. Except for the little kids, but none of them were making much noise. Most of the men were ignoring everything the best they could, but some of the younger guys had stepped out front. Lisa figured they'd learned self-defense the hard way.

That didn't have to happen for the dozen or so women listening to what they could do to protect themselves in case of emergency. She'd already spoken about listening to your instincts, being loud and what she meant by that, which had scared the bejesus out of several doctors and patients. "So, if you don't do anything else, please get a whistle. The loudest one you can find. Get used to wearing it all the time. And even if it feels like you're overreacting, if the little voice in your head tells you something's wrong, listen! It can save your life."

Valeria, who'd joined the group along with a few other nurses, said, "My instincts say you need to teach us a lot more."

That was met by a lot of nodding heads and a few claps.

"I'm not a teacher. I went over the places you can sign up for classes. I'll type it up and hand out flyers, okay?"

"That's a fine idea, but there aren't classes in this neighborhood. There was a free one at the YMCA, but that closed," Valeria said. "What we need now is to learn those moves you just talked about. The basics. Shouldn't take all that long. One afternoon, I imagine. And I know just the place. It's about four blocks from here. Peterson Park."

"That's great, but I can't teach it." Lisa wasn't going to back down on this. She already had a job and a volunteering commitment. "A good course on self-defense runs for weeks."

Mrs. W.'s voice shushed the mumbling. "Honey, after what we seen you do, there ain't nobody gonna teach us how to do all that krave magrave jitsu stuff but you."

Twenty minutes later, Lisa caved.

DANIEL CAUGHT UP to Lisa in the lounge. Still trying to forget the feel of her in his arms, he focused completely on pouring his coffee, not even daring to look at her. "I'd really prefer we go someplace that isn't a busy coffeehouse. I know a restaurant that's quiet and private. So, dinner?" He glanced around the lounge, making sure they were still alone. "No one will bother us. Will you think about it?"

She nodded. Grabbed the last glazed doughnut and left the lounge.

AT 12:30, LISA texted Daniel while she was in the last stall in the bathroom. It was the safest place in the building, not that anyone would give a damn about her typing a text message. Lunch? The pizza place on 3rd?

While finishing the filing, wearing gloves this time, her gut told her dinner was dangerous. Despite what had happened yesterday, they had to slow down with…whatever they were doing. Besides, he needed to understand she wasn't going to sleep with him tonight. Maybe never again. But definitely not tonight.

"WOULD YOU EXCUSE me for a moment?" Daniel said. "I need to answer this." The nurse nodded. After reading Lisa's counteroffer, he played his next hand. Someone could see us at the pizza place. I can pick you up and get you home if we go to dinner. He put his phone away hoping she'd agree.

No texts came while he examined his next patient. Then Daniel was off to a meeting with the financial manager of the clinic. Maybe talking about budgets would prepare him for the next round in this most interesting negotiation. He'd back down the minute she signaled he was going too far, but damn, he hoped she said yes. The restaurant he had in mind was excellent, and it was very close to his town house.

DANIEL STOOD UP as the host brought Lisa to the table. She'd insisted on meeting him there at 8:00, and he had to admit, seeing her like this was worth the wait. Her light blue dress was sleeveless and showed off her amazing figure. Heads turned as she passed tables of diners. He wasn't surprised. Lisa was a stunner. That her beauty seemed effortless added to her appeal.

He helped her to her seat, sneaking a sniff of her honey-scented hair. Wishing he could taste her lips, he sat across from her. She'd gotten comfortable, placing her small purse on the table along with her hands. "Fancy place."

"It's close to home. I've been coming here for years. Though I haven't been in since— Well, not for a while." He watched her gaze sweep across the simple but elegant room, surprised at how much he wanted to impress her. "They have an excellent wine list. Though if you'd prefer a cocktail first…"

"Wine sounds great, if you'd do the honors."

By the time they'd ordered and had their wine, he felt more relaxed, and he thought she was, too. "It was nice of you to agree to teach the defense class."

"As if I had a choice."

"No, I suppose you didn't. You've gotten everyone all fired up. The idea is terrific. It's a tough world for most of our patients." He took another sip of wine. "Want to hear something weird?"

"I don't know," she said. "Do I?"

He chuckled at her suspicious frown. "I don't think I've ever been this nervous on a date before."

She blinked. "Well, this isn't a date."

Of course, she was joking, but before he could think of a witty retort, he got distracted by her neatly trimmed nails. They'd scratched his chest yesterday, and he had the marks and other mementos to prove it. Clearing his throat and the memory, he asked, "What would you call it?"

She shrugged. "A coffee substitute." She stopped to take a deep breath. "What happened yesterday—we can never do that again."

Her stern tone did something wicked to his libido. But of course she was right. They couldn't. Having sex at the clinic was one of the stupidest things he'd ever done. And he'd done plenty over the years. "You're absolutely right. It was completely unprofessional. We can never have sex again," he said. "Not in the clinic."

Her gaze snapped back to his, her lips slightly parted and her eyes wide with disbelief. "I'm not joking."

"Neither am I. Don't get me wrong. Yesterday was an astonishing surprise. With the single exception of the venue, it was also one of the best things that's happened to me in far too long. Although quickies aren't normally my thing." He paused just as the waiter approached with their starters. "I like to take my time."

She opened her mouth but promptly closed it again. The awkward smile she gave the waiter made Daniel want to grin. He held it in check, although it wasn't easy watching her trying to appear as if nothing at all was amiss. The soft lighting nearly hid her faint blush. She kept her hands under the table, so if she wanted to strangle him he couldn't tell. Her eyes, though… Nothing could temper the fiery blaze aimed at him.

Roberto set chilled pea soup in front of Daniel. "Will there be anything else, Dr. Cassidy?"

"We're fine for now, thank you."

"Enjoy," he said with a slight bow and a glance at Lisa.

After eating most of her scallops ceviche, giving him many quizzical looks in the time it took to finish his appetizer, she said, "You're right. Not at the clinic." He thought she might smile then, but she didn't. Not unless he counted the slight upturn of her beautiful lips. Which he did.

Daniel nodded. With those few words his mood shot through the roof. His place really was close. A short walk. An even shorter cab ride. He wondered what she'd think about having their entrées wrapped to go. His cock had a very definite opinion. He tried to ignore it. Or at least calm it down. "So where did you get your defense training?"

She hesitated and the look in her eyes seemed to point inward, as if the question had been somehow out of line. Daniel hoped like hell she hadn't changed her mind.

"I used to be a cop," she said. "In another life."

Now it was his turn to pause. "Really?" He let that digest. She didn't fit his notion of what a cop should look like, but after seeing her in action, it made sense. "When was that?"

"As I said, in another life," she murmured, her lashes sweeping her cheeks. "It's not something I like to talk about."

God, how he understood. There were certainly conversations he never wanted to have. His curiosity wasn't going to go away anytime soon, but he wasn't about to push. "The first time I came to this restaurant, I was seven, I think. It had just opened. My dad ordered oysters on the half shell, so naturally, I did, too, although I only had the vaguest idea what they were."

"Oh, no," she said.

"To say the least." Their dishes were collected, more wine was poured, but he barely noticed anything that wasn't Lisa.

"I waited until I saw how he prepared the horrible things with a shake of hot sauce and a squirt of lemon. He carefully loosened the slimy beasts with his spoon, then leaned back and boom, down the hatch."

"Did you…?"

"Of course I did. I wasn't about to let him or my brother think I was a chicken. It was the worst idea, and I was sick later that night, but I finished all six. I've never eaten oysters again."

"I don't blame you. You were only seven. Why didn't your dad stop you?"

He shrugged. "I suppose it was some kind of lesson, but I will never do that to my kids. Anyway, your turn."

She started a tale of getting mixed up in her big brother's treasure-hunting adventure and how that had led to his ultimate career.

Daniel was still floating through the evening. He was with the most beautiful woman in Manhattan, who also was easy to talk to, laughed in all the right places and told a great story.

Time flew. He barely remembered eating his entrée. All he could think about was how much he'd needed this. Needed someone like Lisa to remind him life still had joy in it.

Too soon their dinner was almost over, and so was the bottle of wine. Maybe that was why he said, "I used to think I knew what I wanted. I'm not sure anymore."

Lisa's hand paused with her drink halfway to her mouth. She blinked several times. He looked away, wishing he'd never said that. He'd put her in an awkward position. They barely knew each other and she'd ducked out of saying anything too personal to him.

"I don't know. Zombie hunting is a burgeoning field. I see those documentaries all the time. Like *Supernatural* and *True Blood*. I think you'd do really well."

He laughed, thankful as hell she'd saved the conversation. He'd like to blame the wine for his loose tongue, but… No. He definitely blamed the wine.

LISA APPRECIATED THE owner and chef of the restaurant coming over to speak to Daniel, but she still resented the intrusion. This coffee substitute was turning out to be the best. She'd never seen Daniel more relaxed. It looked good on him.

Chef Earnhardt was all smiles as he paid particular attention to Lisa. "Enjoying your meal?"

"Very much," she said. "Everything's been outstanding. Thank you."

"My pleasure." The chef turned to Daniel. "And you. My friend. I was so sorry to hear about your father. He was a brilliant and unique man. I'll miss him."

"Thank you, Terrance," Daniel replied in his Dr. Cassidy voice.

"I imagine it helps that you're working with Warren at the Center. Family is so important."

Lisa stiffened. She knew this was a hot-button issue for Daniel. He wasn't working there for a reason. What that was, she had no idea, but his hand had left hers as quickly as Daniel had left her standing in the lounge the day they'd met.

"Family," he said with a broken smile. "Family *is* important."

Earnhardt took a step back. "If I may be so bold," he said to Lisa alone, "I would like to bring you a dessert. Something off the menu."

"I'd love that," she said in between quick glances at Daniel. "Thank you."

The chef went back to his kitchen, but he'd left an air of embarrassment and sadness behind. Maybe if she understood why Daniel had been triggered she could say something that would help. "Are you okay?"

He nodded, even though he wasn't. He barely looked at her. Although he'd seemed utterly lost while the chef had spoken to her, he now looked angry. He clenched his jaw, relaxed and then did it again. Lisa was sorry she'd agreed to the dessert. Daniel wanted to leave; she could see it in his face.

"My father died three months ago," he stated, as if for the record. "It was a shock. He was a neurologist. Brilliant as advertised. He's why I became a neurologist."

"I heard from one of the nurses that your specialty is needed quite often at the clinic."

He gave her a crooked grin and seemed to relax a little at her attempt to change the subject. "My brother, Warren, works at the Madison Avenue Neurological Center. I'll be working there, too, at some point."

"That'll be quite a change from Moss Street."

"It will," he said and downed the rest of his wine.

Dessert arrived, a light concoction that tasted like honey and spring. She offered some to Daniel, but he told her to eat up. She only finished it not to be rude. He did smile a lot as she ate, but the mood had shifted.

Dinner ended on a melancholy note when he walked her to a taxi. She hadn't even tried to argue that she could catch the subway home. "I'm sorry," he said, after paying the driver. "It's something I don't like to talk about."

"No need to apologize. I really get it. More than most people, I imagine," she said and met his eyes. "I'm still glad we did this. It was a lot better than coffee."

"I'll see you…?"

She started to shrug. The look on his face stopped her.

She knew that look. It came from drowning without any water nearby. It was feeling sick at the thought of being alone. A look that she wouldn't wish on anyone. Yet she couldn't see how to offer help or comfort. Not without getting pulled in too deep herself.

She cleared her throat. "I'll probably be at the clinic in the next day or so."

"I'll see you then." He hesitated, staring into her eyes for a long moment, and then opened the cab door.

After sliding in, she looked at him. "Don't you want to ride?"

He shook his head. "I'm two blocks away. The walk will do me good."

She smiled and nodded. As soon as the driver pulled away, she looked back at Daniel. He just stood there, his hands in his pockets.

Lisa wished she'd at least kissed him.

8

DANIEL HAD PUT her in a cab an hour ago. But he wasn't tired. He thought about going for a walk. Exhausting himself. He sure as hell shouldn't have another drink.

The night had started out so well. Why had he let her go? He'd seen the possibility for more in Lisa's eyes. They could have been naked by now. Or not. Maybe they would have just talked.

The way they'd left things was certainly open for interpretation. Aside from his mood swing, he was certain that sex was the thing they both agreed on.

Damn it, he really hated that he'd let her see him like that. Terrance was only an acquaintance, for God's sake. Why the hell was an acquaintance invested in him going to the Center? It was bad enough with Warren calling and Eve giving him lectures. Now he had to be careful where he ate?

He got up, anxious, fidgety. Practically did a whole tour of the brownstone. It was clean as a whistle. Nothing out of place. He'd had a pleasant relationship as a child with Uncle Frank. He'd been a plane fanatic. Who wouldn't have liked that? That had been it, though. But Uncle Frank had still left the brownstone to him. Because Warren was the oldest. He got the family home.

Daniel had inherited the place four years ago, moved in after he returned from his residency at Johns Hopkins, but he hadn't done much to make it his own. Instead he'd jumped into his fellowship at Mount Sinai. He'd managed to buy a new bed, but mostly, Daniel had ignored everything else.

The last woman he'd had in here had told him how iconic it was. What she meant was old-fashioned. Daniel didn't care. His home didn't have to be a showcase or even an extension of himself. Another way he was unlike his father and Warren.

Damn it, he should have selected a restaurant he'd never been to before. Daniel stood at the wet bar. Between the bottles he could see broken snips of his face on the mirror back. The man staring at him looked drawn and tired, certainly too tired to make any decisions. If he had another drink he was going to call Lisa, and that was the one thing he shouldn't do.

He left the bar without a drink, still feeling restless. He ran his fingers over the unread hardbound volumes on his shelves. Another of the hundred things he'd meant to do and hadn't.

Like go to Dad's place. Warren's place. That sounded wrong, and if he saw any of Warren's things…

"For God's sake," he mumbled, pulling his cell phone out of his pocket. "Grow a pair." He went to the big window facing the park. It was beautiful out there now.

Closing his eyes, he took a deep breath. This wasn't like him. He wasn't a procrastinator.

His father used to tell people his youngest was born a neurologist. Daniel had been so proud he'd studied his ass off to graduate with honors in medical school. All during his residency. Jesus. He'd barely looked up. But he'd been happy. Pursuing the one thing he'd always wanted.

Until he'd finished his fellowship. Damn, he wished he'd never had that dinner with his father. But then, maybe his unease had started earlier; he didn't know anymore. Though he'd never minded that his father's career was the most important thing in his life.

Frankly, Daniel hadn't known anything else. Dad was a brilliant man. But he lived and breathed medicine and the Center he'd founded. Nothing could compete with the high he got from his work. Not his wife, not mistresses, not his children.

He had one son who was faithfully following in his footsteps. No life outside of medicine. Obsessed with image and accolades. The son who hadn't been born a neurologist.

Given how their father had clearly favored his youngest son, it seemed odd that Warren had still modeled his life after Dad. Daniel had no idea if Warren used conferences to meet women like their father had.

Daniel had finally seen all those things, but they hadn't mattered. Because he'd believed his father was truly devoted to medicine. And not his own ego. His family—except for bragging purposes—and everything else in life were insignificant.

Was it any wonder Daniel wanted to think it through? To stop and examine his life? Yes, he loved the work, but that wasn't all he wanted. He wanted to be married, and he wanted a wife, not a trophy.

Honestly, Warren wasn't the problem. He was often a prick, but he wasn't the one at fault. If anything, Daniel had kept his distance because he'd felt bad for him. But it was time to move forward. He hit speed dial. His chest tightened as he listened to the phone ring. It went to voice mail.

He opened his mouth to leave a message, but he had no idea what to say. Not one thought. He'd try again tomorrow.

He stared at his cell. He had her number. But it was 11:30. They weren't at the late-night-call stage. Screw it. He hit speed dial.

She answered right away.

"Did I wake you?" he asked.

"No." She hesitated. "I'm sitting in a cab outside your place."

SHE WAS OUTSIDE? JESUS. His heart rate spiked. Daniel pulled the door open and met her on the porch. The second they were inside, Lisa was in his arms. Touching her, stroking her back, the curve of her waist, the lush bottom cheeks he could cover with both hands. This was what he'd wanted but hadn't been able to ask.

He walked her to his bedroom, kissing her the whole time, drinking in her moans, letting out more than his share. Even if they'd bumped into something, he doubted he could've stopped kissing her. God, he wanted everything. To see her naked, to lean over her and look down into that gorgeous face.

He pulled back a step next to the bed.

Lisa leaned up again, but then she opened her eyes. "Oh. We're in your bedroom."

He nodded, waited for her to check out his California king and the open en suite door. It was tempting to keep going, to make the rest of the world disappear. "Is this okay?"

"It's beautiful. And big. I'm not used to big houses."

"No, I meant…is it okay that I want to strip that dress right off you." He nipped her earlobe. "See if you taste like honey when you come."

"Oh, that." She smiled. "As long as you have condoms, then yes. It's okay. Better than o—"

He hadn't been kidding. A moment later, her blue dress was off, tossed to the overstuffed love seat near the wall. "Goddamn it."

Lisa covered her bare breasts. "What's wrong?"

"Nothing." Why was she covering the most beautiful pair of breasts he'd ever seen?

"You said, 'Goddamn it.'"

"Out loud?"

She grinned. "Out loud."

"Sorry about that," he said, gently moving her arms to her sides. "The problem is I want to do everything at once, and that's not possible."

"I'll give you a hint. You're wearing a lot of clothes."

"Doesn't matter. We can take care of that after I've…" He bent down and took her right nipple between his lips. Her breasts were small, with stunning pink areolae and nipples that stuck out like erasers. She gasped when he swirled his tongue around the stiff bud, then released it and blew soft breaths.

"Oh, that feels unbelievable."

"You're so sensitive."

"I would probably have scratched your back if you weren't wearing a dinner jacket."

He looked up, but didn't straighten. "Tell you what. I'll take off every stitch if you make sure these amazing nipples of yours stay hard and ripe."

"Deal," she said. Before he could leave with a nice little suck, Lisa's hand moved in and she covered it up.

"Such a stickler for the rules." He straightened and got busy undressing. The moment his jacket came off, she commenced with her part of the bargain. Damn it, he should have started with his trousers instead, because now his erection was painfully hard as he watched her tease her nipples with her fingertips, pull them, tweak them so hard she winced and moaned at the same time.

He toed off his shoes and stripped as quickly as he could, just dropping everything to the floor. "You're beautiful," he whispered, stepping toward her. "Especially when you're flushed and gasping."

She lowered her hands, her breath catching, when he got close enough to lick the side of her neck, to feel her extended nipples graze his chest.

He'd thought about asking her to leave her panties on, and taking them off with his teeth, but he couldn't wait to touch her there. If her nipples were this hard, what would he find between her legs?

He kissed her, but he also put his hands on her sides and lifted her, only to put her down on the side of the bed. Then he kept moving forward with his body, gripping her arms to lay her down. When he finally pulled back, her eyes were so dilated, he could barely see any of the blue he liked so much.

Although this look might be his favorite now. Her chest and neck were flushed with arousal. As he moved slowly down, he teased her left nipple for as long as he was able to keep the awkward position—knees bent, hands gripping the bedspread, his cock the only other part of his body to touch her, leaving a slight trail of pre-come that said a lot about his patience.

He blew on her nipple, and watched it tighten, but then he was on the move again. Finally, his knees met the hardwood floor. Before he removed her panties, he ran his thumb down the damp crotch.

Her thighs quivered. "Stop teasing, Daniel. I mean it."

Daniel smiled. "I thought this time we'd take it slow."

"Fine. But— No, not fine. I'm ready to pop and if you don't—"

He stopped her when he whipped down her tiny bikini panties, and put his mouth directly on her swollen pink pussy.

The command turned into a high squeal. Her breathing changed as he sucked on her clitoris. He flicked it with the tip of his tongue and slid two fingers inside her.

God, she was moaning like she might die. If she didn't come quickly, he might "pop" himself. He quickly slipped on the condom, and then his fingers were back where they belonged. Rubbing her, teasing her, spreading her folds wide so her clitoris was as plump as her nipples, but completely utterly different on his tongue.

Her legs went over his shoulders and her heels gripped his back. Excellent. He'd meant to do that himself, but he liked that she'd gone for it on her own.

He kept on flicking that beautiful nub as he rose until his lower legs were his only support. This way, he was able to grab her by her arms and pull her up. It meant chasing her clit, but then Lisa clutched his shoulders.

"Holy… If you stop, I'll kill you. I'm right there. Right there—"

She almost knocked him to the floor when she came. It was fantastic. And she was gorgeous. Before she finished quaking, he positioned his cock at her entrance and thrust all the way into her with one stroke.

He moaned, she cried out, and in a maddeningly short time, he came. The last thing he saw before he had to close his eyes was Lisa's face. She looked perfect.

THE PARK WAS lovely at this time of the morning. The case Lisa was working required her to make contact with a particular nanny who brought her ward here daily. And all Lisa could think about was last night.

She'd meant to comfort Daniel. To be there for whatever

was making him so distraught. Turned out sex had been
the answer. Which, honestly, worked out for both of them.
They hadn't needed to talk—well, not too much. From his
admission at dinner, she still knew more about him than
felt comfortable. That was why she'd left in the wee hours
while he'd been sleeping.

With a jolt, she looked around at the other benches that
lined the playground area. The nanny she was waiting for
hadn't arrived yet.

Her coffee was now lukewarm. Thinking about last night
as if she'd been an observer wasn't helping much. She understood how brave Daniel was to share anything personal
with a relative stranger. She got how it felt to have the life
you'd planned turn to ashes. Her chest tightened and a lump
came to her throat, just like it had the night before. Perhaps
she wasn't as neutral as she'd thought.

She liked him. A lot. She wondered how he'd reacted
to the note she'd left him.

God, she hated these divorce cases with a passion, especially when she was sleep deprived. There was so much
waiting. So much time to think. Isabel Charles still hadn't
shown up. Every day the nanny brought her ward to this
Upper West Side park at exactly 11:30 so little Alice could
play with her friends while Isabel swapped gossip with the
other nannies. So where the hell was she?

Lisa had dressed for the part. She'd worn a sundress,
not too revealing and not too sheer. Her sandals were upscale and going on her expense report, but the shoes in her
large tote were much more useful Skechers, which were
what most of the other nannies changed into just before
they headed home.

If she'd been smart, she would have started up a conversation with some of the nannies already there. That would
have kept Lisa occupied. Two other benches held three, and

another two, and then there she was, alone. This was the bench Isabel preferred. Typically, she sat here until around noon, when Isabel's friend Carrie arrived.

Something needed to keep her attention away from Daniel. Even the dinner had been mostly terrific. They'd laughed and swapped childhood stories, and she'd felt more intoxicated from that than the wine. She'd felt like her old self. But really, the flirty, tingling, heart-pounding crap had to stop.

Why had she agreed to teach self-defense to a bunch of semi-strangers? Yes, it had been Lisa Pine who'd agreed, but Lisa McCabe was the one who had the most to lose. She should have disappeared days before the junkie had shown up.

She needed to stop volunteering, that was all. Tell them her time was needed elsewhere. She'd miss that, too. Being with people again had felt great. More than great.

Okay, that was a problem. Her life before Moss Street was just the way she liked it. Private. Quiet. Uneventful.

There wasn't room for anyone else. Not even Daniel.

For pity's sake, could she not go two minutes without having him pop into her thoughts? Damn it, this thing with him was stirring up emotions that were better left alone. Despite all the rules she'd set up in her head, she had… feelings for him. She hadn't wanted to go home last night. She'd wanted to wake up next to him.

Just as she was about to get up and stretch, she saw the nanny. Isabel had arrived with the sound track of a sobbing five-year-old.

"It's all right, Alice." Isabel put her bag down on the far end of Lisa's bench. "Mommy and Daddy were just having a discussion. Remember when we talked about discussions? Hmm? That they're loud, but no one wants to hurt you?"

Lisa felt bad for Isabel, really, but this was also a good

opportunity. She checked that her recorder was in her pocket and said, "Can I help?"

Isabel looked over at her. "She'll eventually wear herself out. Where's yours?"

"Don't have one now. I'm looking. Just finished working for a family with three-year-old twins. The father left them high and dry, and Mom had to start working. Grandma flew in from Ohio."

"Oh, that sucks." Isabel lifted Alice to her chest and sat down. Rocking the still-screaming child, she turned to look at Lisa. "Where was that?"

"Columbus Circle."

"Ah. I'm Central Park West. I think there might be someone in the building who's looking. Who did your résumé?"

"Althea? At the Nanny Connection?"

"Oh, she did mine. She actually found me this job. Pay's great, but the fighting is really getting old."

Lisa turned on the recorder and moved a little closer. "It's awful when the parents are having it out. Hell on the kids."

"You're telling me." Isabel sighed, patted Alice's back. "He's not bad, but she's like something out of a horror movie."

"I had just the opposite."

"Did he get high, too? I'm pretty sure she's addicted to Adderall."

"No, but he drank a lot. They used to put all their empty bottles in other people's recycling."

Isabel nodded, and from her look, Lisa inferred the mother drank in addition to her addiction.

"I keep thinking," Lisa said, "that they'd fallen in love once. They'd liked each other once upon a time. Enough to want a life together. What happened?"

Isabel gave her a long cynical look and laughed. "You must be new at this."

"What do you mean?"

"Come on, you know how it is. Everything's flowers and unicorns in the beginning. You think you know a person." She shrugged. "Doesn't take too long for their true colors to start showing. Having kids just makes it show earlier."

Lisa closed her eyes for a moment. When she got her bearings, she opened them again. She understood, all right. So how on earth could she have forgotten for even a minute the most important lesson she'd ever learned? She'd thought she knew Tess better than anyone except her brother. Turned out Lisa hadn't known a thing. And now she imagined she knew Daniel?

She barely knew herself.

9

DANIEL KEPT CHECKING his cell phone. Of course Lisa hadn't called. Why would she? Last night was last night. Today she was busy. Like him. He had no business thinking about her while he was at the clinic examining patients.

He still couldn't believe she'd been sitting outside in a cab.

Every time he had a spare moment alone, his thoughts went to her. She'd been so beautiful in that blue dress. Even better without it. He'd been upset about the note she'd left, although the apple had been a nice touch. Thing was, he'd wanted to wake up to her. Which was nuts. She'd brought nothing with her. No change of clothes or anything, and she had to go to work. Her leaving wasn't a statement about their future.

At least he hoped not.

While he was still annoyed that the chef had talked about Warren and the clinic, he'd recognized, albeit slowly and with great regret, that the problem was his, and that it would continue to be a problem until he figured out what he really wanted.

That was why he was still at the clinic. He didn't know which path to take, not anymore. For now, he liked being at the clinic for more reasons than he cared to share. He was reasonably sure no one knew about his father's outrageous plans but himself. That was why it was hard to talk to Warren.

It wasn't all just about that, though, He'd always known that his wild oats would be cut off the moment he graduated. But for now, the free clinic was a safe harbor. Since he wasn't working at the Center, he didn't feel the pressure to put on the straitjacket of outward decorum. He would never in a million years have had sex with a volunteer in the Madison Avenue Center. Of course, he wouldn't have met Lisa, either.

THE MINUTE LISA had recorded enough information, she'd left the park, hoping the nanny never found out she'd been a part of her boss's upcoming divorce.

As she walked down the steps to the subway, Lisa thought about how much time she'd spent at the clinic. How easy it was to have sex with Daniel, and how simple it would be to fall into another trap. At least she had this job. Although she wished she wasn't stuck with these awful divorce cases so often. They were all boring as hell. Divorces. Custody cases. Runaway dads.

She knew they paid her salary, but she was being wasted. Before her life had imploded, she'd been thinking of asking her captain for undercover work. She knew damn well Logan could use a woman for that sort of thing. She could do it. After what had happened at the clinic, she knew she still had massive skills. No more filing. No more mindless waiting. There wouldn't be time or the energy to think about Daniel. Or sex. Or anything that might get her into trouble. Boredom was her main problem.

Anyway, it was time she moved on to meatier cases. It

had been sixteen months since Tess had stolen her life. All she had to do was convince Logan she was ready.

She boarded her train and stared out the window, trying to decide how she should approach her brother. Fifteen minutes later she pulled out her cell phone, hoping he had a few minutes for her. She knew he was in the middle of coordinating an international sex-trafficking sting. From what she'd overheard, there would be a lot of politicians making headlines next week. It was exactly the kind of case she would've loved to be involved with.

"What's up?" Logan had caught the call on the first ring. Good. Sounded as if he was in the hurry-up-and-wait stage.

"Have a few minutes?"

"Sure."

"I was thinking—"

"Uh-oh."

"Come on. I'm serious. I was thinking it's about time I got involved in some of the more interesting cases."

"Meaning?"

"I've got skills, Logan. You know I do."

"Okay. That's something we'll talk about later."

She'd heard the sigh he tried to hide. "You do know you're not Dad, right?"

"I'm not Mom, either. Hold on, I've got another call."

While she waited as Logan took the other call on his landline, she put him on speaker, so she'd know when he was back to her, but she didn't really listen in on his conversation. Luckily, there were only three people in her subway car, and in accordance with the Official Sanctified Rules of the Subway Riders of New York, no one gave a shit about her or her phone. She was free to get her points in order in case Logan wanted to argue.

First of all, she'd taken down that junkie without a moment's hesitation. Which Logan didn't know about because she'd been embarrassed to tell him she was volunteering at the clinic. Even though Heather had taken a pass on Daniel, Logan might not see Lisa swooping in as 100 percent kosher.

But it wouldn't matter if Lisa Pine never went back to the clinic.

The idea alone made her stomach turn over. That meant not seeing Daniel again. Which, she admitted, was mostly the point. Okay, precisely the point. A more challenging job might distract her from doing something stupid. She couldn't afford to lose herself again.

And what about the self-defense class she'd agreed to teach? Was she willing to let all those women down?

Christ, this was getting complicated.

"Lisa?"

She took her phone off speaker. "I'm here."

"Tell me what's going on."

She knew that tone of voice. The subway stopped and she got out. From where she was, Logan's office was two streets away. If he got hardheaded she could swing by for a face-to-face instead of going straight home. Let him try looking her in the eye and telling her she wasn't ready to take on more responsibility.

"Lisa?"

"Sorry, subway madness." She took the steps up fast. And practically ran down West Broadway. Thank God for her Skechers. "Hold on a second."

She waited until she'd made it almost a block and caught her breath. Stalling for time, she asked, "What are you doing for dinner later?"

"Seriously?" Logan laughed. "You know what I'm working on. In fact—"

"Wait." She crossed against the red light and ignored

the taxi that nearly clipped her. "I need more," she said. "I don't expect to drop most of the ordinary stuff, but I'd like to add some tougher cases."

"Define *tougher*."

"Oh, I don't know—something I can't do in my sleep."

"Look, Lisa—" His landline rang, and she could almost smell his relief. "I have to take another call. Let's talk—"

"I'll wait. No problem."

This time he didn't try to hold back his sigh. If he pretended to hang up on her by mistake, she'd show him just how capable she was of taking down 195 pounds of hard muscle.

She jogged the last half a block, then inserted her card key into the office door lock. She nodded at Mike, who had the sorry task of acting as receptionist when he wasn't directly working on a case or a temp didn't show. Now, though, he pretty much ignored her and went back to whatever he was doing.

"Okay, I'm back," Logan said and didn't so much as blink when she entered his office. Of course he was surprised, and maybe irritated, but he didn't show it. He was a master at hiding what he was feeling. He nodded at one of his guest chairs, but she was too antsy to sit. "What brought this on?"

"I was at the clinic the day before yesterday when—"

"The clinic as in the free clinic?"

She nodded. "All my work here was taken care of. And I've started volunteering there…" She cleared her throat. "But I don't think I'm gonna do that anymore, so it's a moot point."

"Why?"

Sitting down in the huffiest way she knew how, she said, "Sometimes you annoy the crap out of me." She would have put her feet up on the edge of his desk if she wasn't wearing a dress.

"Sometimes? I'll work on that."

She sighed. "This is important to me."

"All right." He sat up straighter and folded his hands on his meticulous desk. "Go ahead. I'm listening."

"I walked in on a situation. All I could see was this guy aiming a shaky Glock 17 at one of the staff and holding on to this kid. The temperature of the room was in the stratosphere, so I figured he'd been there for a while…"

She stood up again, walked to the window. "I dropped my purse. He turned around. Called me Barbie, then—"

When she looked at her brother there was concern in his eyes. She knew she sounded hyper but that might not be a bad thing. "He was high. It wasn't difficult to secure the weapon and take him down. The police picked him up about five minutes later."

Logan had put his blank face on. He wasn't supposed to use that on her. "I'm glad it turned out okay," he said.

She walked back to the chair. It wasn't easy holding in her frustration. He clearly didn't understand how much she needed the upgrade.

"Seems like you're still wound pretty tight."

"You know how it is." She leaned forward. "How the adrenaline takes over. Just because I've been lying low for a while—"

"Over a year."

"Logan. Knock that off. What I'm saying is, I may be rusty, but I haven't got amnesia. I knew what to do, and I did it safely. Remember how I used to tell you my biggest advantage was that I was small?"

"Course I do. I haven't got amnesia, either. I can see the takedown brought a lot of satisfaction with it. But—"

"I wasn't through," she said. "What I want to do while

I'm getting back to prime is build a new identity for my-self. No help from you. Not yet. I want to be as thorough as I can, straight back to a birth certificate, driver's license, the whole nine. Meanwhile, I continue taking the easy stuff, and I start working out. Hard."

His eyes narrowed. "Why a new identity at all?"

"I don't think it's an advantage to go by McCabe."

He leaned back, his gaze unwavering. "You're not ready."

"How can you say that? You, of all people, should understand I need to get back into the game."

"Yep, I do get it. That's how I know you're not ready." He ignored her exasperated sigh. "You've got time, Lisa. So take it. Do your volunteer work, get laid once in a while, ease back into life. The job will still be here."

"Logan, damn it, you're not being fair. You've acclimated to civilian life just fine."

His brows rose in disbelief and hurt. "Do you really not remember how I was after Afghanistan?"

Shame caught her by the gut. Of course she remembered. He'd been a wreck and trying desperately to prove he wasn't. "I'm sorry. Of course I do. I don't think you're right about me, but I'll play it safe for a while longer. I'm going to work on getting back to black-belt condition."

"Great idea. And so is your volunteering. You spent a long time isolating yourself." He leaned forward and gave her a smile that reminded her just how much he loved her. "Stay in shape. We'll see what happens in six months or so."

She flinched at the time frame, but she wasn't going to bitch. What he wanted to see was proof that she was ready mentally and physically and that was what he'd get. "Fine." She stood up, anxious now, to leave.

Logan stood, too. He came over to her side of the desk

and put an arm around her shoulders. "I'm serious about the volunteering. Doing good things for other people can be empowering. Take it easy on yourself." He walked her to his office door. "And make good use of that doctor of yours."

She didn't shove him away, but she did give him the finger, which only made him laugh. Her phone rang. It was a text from Valeria. Twenty-two people had signed up for her self-defense class. Now they wanted to know which day worked for her.

She gave up. Fine. She'd teach the damn class. But before she could respond, another text came through. It was from Daniel.

She smiled all the way to the street corner.

10

LISA WAS BUSY typing up notes from what she'd learned from the nanny this morning. It rattled her that she hadn't remembered the last third of their conversation. If Lisa hadn't recorded the whole thing she would've been screwed. And even more angry with herself for this stupid obsession with Daniel.

She glanced at her cell phone. It was 6:00. He'd be calling her in the next ten minutes or so, right after he finished up at the clinic. They'd texted twice and then agreed upon a time when they could talk. She expected he'd bring up her leaving last night, though she wished he wouldn't. The more she knew about Daniel and his demons, the stickier things would get between them. And since she hadn't decided what to do about him or volunteering at the clinic, it was best they stayed away from personal issues.

This was so crazy. It should be a simple decision, a complete no-brainer. So why had she gone back and forth a thousand times since she'd left Logan's office? Whether she stayed in it for the sex, or cut ties with Daniel right after she did the self-defense thing, the story could end only one way. His true colors would bleed out like a wound. Ironically so would hers. When he found out she'd lied about her name and why she'd been at the clinic…why would he stay?

But none of that had to happen if it was just sex. Sex with no private confession, no expectations, nothing too real. So why not just sex?

Was it ever just sex? He already knew she'd been a cop. However inadvertently, he'd told her about his father, his brother, the Center. No, in the end he'd break her heart.

Oh, God.

That kind of thinking was what really got her in trouble. They didn't have that kind of relationship, so everybody's heart was going to stay intact. No worries there as long as they both understood the ground rules.

She blinked at the bleary computer screen. Got up for another soda. Her apartment was so tiny she made it to the fridge in five steps. She really needed to go shopping soon, although her shopping lists were very tiny. Thank God for corner bodegas with their salad bars and ethnic eats.

Oddly, she didn't resent that she could only afford this broom closet. A place with more natural light would've been nice but she was managing just fine.

Her phone rang and she quickly gulped down the mouthful of soda.

"Hello, Dr. Cassidy," she said, glancing at the time. "You're wrapping up early."

"Hey, hold on a second. Another call."

Lisa took another sip of soda, but he was back before she swallowed.

"Just Eve telling me my brother's in France at a conference. Anyway, I'm not wrapping up early. Just the opposite. I've been running behind all day. Completely your fault, by the way."

"What did I do?" Lisa spun around in her office chair,

feeling the tension leave her body. His tone of voice was upbeat, friendly.

"The kids are all pretending to be Bruce Lee. Hector totally lost control of the waiting area."

Lisa laughed. "God, I hope you're kidding."

"Let's just say a boy who came in for allergies ended up being treated for a bloody nose and sprained wrist."

She groaned. "That's terrible. I don't know what to say."

Daniel chuckled. "Hey, at the end of the day, the clinic and everyone involved came out ahead. Did you hear about the guy you took down? According to the police, Kroger wasn't just a meth addict. He cooked the stuff in a basement three blocks from a middle school."

"Valeria texted something to that effect. I hope you didn't mention anything about my being a cop?" The second the words were out of her mouth she wished she could call them back.

"No, Lisa," he said quietly. "I wouldn't do that."

"I do know. Reflex. Sorry."

"No problem. So, about the list of folks who signed up for your class…"

"Yeah?"

"Add two more."

"Twenty-four? Jesus. I don't know if I can even speak loud enough, let alone have all of them work on moves." She wasn't kidding. "Are you one of the latecomers?"

Daniel laughed. "That's a big no."

"Afraid I'll show you up?"

"Oh, hell, that's a given."

Lisa laughed again. Why was this man so easy to talk to? Doubts, fears, everything seemed to drift away.

"I spoke to Eve yesterday and told her about what happened. Amazingly no one else got to her first. She was speechless."

"I bet," Lisa said, careful to keep her voice even. She knew Eve wasn't a fan of hers and that was okay.

"You don't understand. I've known Eve for ages. She always has a comeback. I told her she should go to your self-defense class."

"Will she?"

"I doubt it. But she's glad everyone else is going. Have you decided which evening's going to work for you?"

"Definitely not tomorrow. Not only do I have to get up at a horrifying hour the following morning, I need some time to put together a plan for the class."

Silence lasted long enough to give her a bad feeling before he said, "Hey, I'm sorry if I made you feel uncomfortable last night."

"Stop. I wasn't uncomfortable. I had a great dinner, I loved your stories, and as for the rest, I think you know how much I enjoyed that. I know I left with just a note, but I honestly had to go home. You see? Everything's fine." She took a breath. "No offense, but you need to stop going to restaurants where people know you so well."

"You're absolutely right. McDonald's it is."

She laughed and he did, too. But it didn't escape her attention that she'd ignored an ideal window to tell Daniel she couldn't see him again.

DANIEL FELT BETTER hearing that laugh of hers. "I should be free in an hour. Want to get something to eat?" he asked, hoping she'd say yes, but not counting on it. She did say work was getting intense.

"Tempting as a burger and fries sound, I'm swamped. I'm trying to finish up a report so I'll have time for the class."

That made perfect sense but he was still disappointed. God, he was behaving like a child. He wanted Lisa all the time. That was new. And not very pleasant. He liked feeling as though he had the upper hand.

"Where are you?" she asked. "It doesn't sound like the clinic."

"I'm out back. There's an alley with a dubious reputation, but I'm at the entrance, so no muggers yet. Also, someone has chickens, because I hear a lot of clucking."

"Oh, man, too bad. That sounds like a terrible place to have phone sex."

He dropped his cell phone but caught it before it hit the ground. "I can throw someone out of an exam room. Won't be a minute."

That laugh again. It made his entire day.

"Nah," she said. "Maybe next time."

He hadn't even known that was exactly what he'd wanted to hear. "You bet. Next time."

THREE DAYS AND A smattering of text messages and phone conversations with Daniel later, Lisa was still a bundle of nerves as she saw the group of women standing on the grass at Peterson Park. It hadn't helped that yesterday she'd worked on a stakeout from just after dawn until midnight, and today her attempt at a nap had mostly been her worrying, only horizontally instead of vertically.

On the plus side, the park looked like a great place to hang. There was a legit baseball diamond complete with stands and lots of trees. Lots of picnic tables, too. Most of them filled with families. Little kids were running around with balloons; a few were crying. There'd been a park near her house when she was a kid, and she remembered the feeling of picnics and innocence. Walking past all that helped her shoulders relax and her chest to stop tightening. Then Valeria saw her and waved and in a blink, the tension returned.

She recognized a lot of folks. Mrs. W. to start with, and nurses she'd met and some fellow volunteers. She didn't know all their names, and when she got closer, she noticed more unfamiliar faces—and there were a lot more than twenty-four. She'd give Valeria grief later.

As she reached the group, she realized that despite his joking around, she'd expected Daniel to be there. The part of her that wasn't scared to pieces was worryingly disappointed.

"Here she is," Valeria said, rocking tight gym shorts and a tattered sleeveless white T that showed off her tats. "For those who haven't met her, this is Lisa Pine. Our resident hero."

Lisa smiled, but it jarred her to hear the phony name. "Hey, everyone," she said, raising her voice. "First, can everyone hear me?"

Someone in the back yelled, "We can't hear you."

A few minutes later Valeria and Josie, an attractive young woman who turned out to be Valeria's way more conservative sister, had the group seated in a half wheel with Lisa as the center spoke. Everyone could hear and see her. After one last big breath, Lisa began.

"Here's the plan," she said. "I'm going to talk to you awhile about listening to your intuition and how to be vocal in an uncomfortable situation. Then I'll answer questions if you have them, and finally I'll show you some basic moves that are easy to master and have saved a lot of women.

"A very smart man who's a leader in the field of self-protection often starts his lectures by asking, 'If you heard there was a weapon proven to prevent most crimes before they happen, would you run out and buy it?' The truth is, you already own it. He calls it 'the gift of fear,' but I prefer to call it 'the gift of intuition.'

"Who here has ever had an experience where you felt

something was off about a person or a situation, but you didn't want to make waves, or look like a jerk, but in the end, things really did go wrong?"

Every hand rose.

"The trick to learning how to trust your intuition is to think of it as your secret weapon. First comes the feeling. It might be a strange sensation in your gut, or the hairs on the back of your neck might stand up. Intuition is your body's early warning system and it's your subconscious at work. In nanoseconds, your awesome brain, which does most of its heavy lifting without you being aware, notes body language, smells something weird, hears a sound that doesn't fit, and makes you feel uncomfortable. The problem isn't that you don't have intuitive feelings and thoughts. It's that we're trained to ignore them. Dismiss them."

Everyone seemed interested. Most of the women were leaning forward, nodding. It felt pretty wonderful, which she hadn't expected. She'd given a few talks at schools when she'd been in uniform. Mostly about stranger danger, but also about drugs or sometimes about being a cop. She'd liked those assignments because she'd felt they made a difference.

The rest of the talk seemed to fly by. At first she asked the ladies to hold their questions, but she gave that up quickly. It wasn't orderly and there was a surprising amount of laughter, but it was all good. Really good. Until she was in the middle of explaining some of the different types of martial arts, and one of the nurses, Beverly, let loose an ear-shattering wolf whistle, exactly the kind they'd discussed during the discussion on harassment. A few others started catcalling at someone behind her.

She spun around and her heart did a little flip. It was Daniel, dressed in normal gym shorts and a short-sleeved T.

He looked good. A little pale, but the definition in his legs made up for it.

The noise settled pretty quickly, though, with everyone still in the semicircle. When Daniel joined Lisa he said, "I'm so glad I didn't disturb the lesson. That would have been terrible."

"Sorry, Dr. Cassidy," Beverly said with a grin. "None of us knew what great legs you had."

"That's amusing, Ms. Chin." He shook his head at all the laughter, then faced Lisa. "I apologize. I really didn't think I'd bring the proceedings to a crashing halt."

"Not at all. You're the vital piece this class was missing."

From the tilt of his head and the half grin, he knew something was up. "Vital piece, huh?"

"I was just about to show some basic self-defense moves, and I needed someone to help me demonstrate them."

"You mean you need a punching bag?" He sounded resigned.

"There won't be any punching. I promise."

He shook his head but she knew he'd be a great sport. So did everyone else, it seemed, by the look of glee on their faces. At the clinic, most everyone treated him with a respectful distance, and he was the only doctor not called by his first name, but he didn't seem to mind the teasing.

Lisa instructed everyone to stand, and while they got to their feet at varying speeds, she took advantage of the moment and whispered to Daniel, "Are you up for this? I shouldn't have volunteered you."

He leaned in close. Close enough that she felt his breath on her cheek. And said, "Bring it."

DANIEL TORE HIS gaze away from Lisa's skintight leggings and bright pink T-back sleeveless shirt. So far he'd managed not to get an erection. But he was definitely playing with fire. The glint of challenge in her steely blue eyes didn't help. Hell, he thought being an hour late was enough. The next half hour was going to be a long one.

He put his doctor smile on. The one he used for meetings. It didn't matter that he wanted to grab Lisa's hand and start running. Nowhere in particular. The first place they found where they could kiss as long as they liked.

Someone laughed about something, bringing him back to reality. To the fact that they were most definitely not alone.

"Dr. Cassidy, could you come over here, please?"

He walked closer to the group and to Lisa. "The most vulnerable places on a body begin at the head. Eyes, ears, nose and neck. Then we move down to the groin, the knees and finally the legs and feet. The position of the attacker and how close or far he is makes all the difference. If he's close and within striking distance, you could strike his nose with your hand or knee him in the junk. Sorry, Doctor."

"No problem," he said, absolutely certain there was a very big problem.

"These are a couple of moves that you should practice," Lisa said, paying him no mind. "Not on a person unless you're in a certified self-defense class. I used to practice in the mirror. It looked stupid, but it worked. Or you can help each other, as long as you remember to move slowly and carefully. Like this."

She grinned at him. "Ready?"

"Depends. What do I do?"

"Stand there—" she pointed at a spot closer to the audience "—and look mean."

He tried, but stopped as soon as he heard laughter. Most of it came from Lisa. She pressed her lips together and then demonstrated how she could poke his eyes out with two fingers, with two knuckles, with a key held in her palm, and finally scratching with her nails. He held his breath through most of it.

"That's a whole lot more ways than I ever thought about," Mrs. Washington said.

"That's going to be true of most of the moves. I want you to think beyond what you've seen on TV. Use what you have. Practice so often, it becomes second nature. Kind of like when you hit that junkie with your purse. I could tell that hadn't been your first time."

That got a laugh and Mrs. Washington beamed. It made Daniel feel more comfortable, as well. He figured the rest would be easier now that he knew what to expect. With the possible exception of her kneeing his junk. Even in slow motion and with no contact, he was going to cringe.

"Don't forget that when you're this distance from your attacker, you might have more than your hand at the ready. You might be able to strike his nose with the base of your hand," she said, demonstrating on him again, "*and* kick his knee or stomp on his foot."

Valeria waved her hand. "If I'm that close, I'm going for the junk. No offense, Dr. Cassidy."

"None taken," he said, smiling. He must remember to bring Valeria coffee and a doughnut every single day.

"Use what you can," Lisa said, her voice carrying easily to everyone. Watching her work was just as extraordinary as the moves she'd put on the junkie.

As she showed the methods of striking his neck and his ear, he thought about what made this class so exceptional. It wasn't the material. It was Lisa's conviction. When she spoke to these women who lived in one of the roughest parts of New York, it was with a belief so heartfelt it couldn't help but inspire. There was so much to admire about her, and yet he couldn't help but wonder again what she'd gone through to have become such a warrior. He would never ask. But he hoped someday she'd tell him.

The rest of the demonstrations went by even more smoothly. He did what she asked, even when she raised her knee, then executed a kick so high, he couldn't bear to think of what it would feel like.

"We're almost at the end," she said. "So I'm going to demonstrate one way to defend yourself if your attacker has you in his grip."

Turning to him, she said, keeping her voice low, "I'd like you to wait until I look away, answering a question or something. Then wrap me in a bear hug. That's both arms around me from behind, your hands clasped at my waist. Okay? Just be aware that this maneuver will be more physical, but I won't hurt you. You'll feel me spreading my knees. Do it with me, if you can. When I drop my weight, you drop, too. Just let it happen. Okay?"

"I'm ready."

"Good." She faced the group again, and sure enough someone's hand came up. But he wasn't about to wait. He wanted this demo over. So he went for it and grabbed Lisa just as she'd asked him to.

There were gasps from the crowd, but before the sound passed, she had shifted her knees, and he'd followed suit. Then she'd dropped her weight forward.

That was when he realized the problem. Not that she couldn't break out of his hold—of course she could. But the way his front was pressed against her backside? Problem. In the junk area.

His mouth, thankfully, was very close to her ear. "Do not," he whispered as strongly as possible, "give me a boner."

She froze. Then she started shaking.

"Quit. Moving."

The shaking got worse, but then she stomped on his

foot, found a finger, pulled it back far enough to cause a twinge, pulled that same arm out as far as she could go, then did a near-miss kick to his elbow joint, then his groin.

Problem. Solved.

She thanked him for being a good sport, and that was when he realized she'd been trying not to laugh out loud. Yet, when she turned her attention to the women in the class, all he could think of was how he could get them both into his bed as quickly as humanly possible.

11

THEY ARRIVED AT Daniel's brownstone in record time. The second they were on the threshold, he pulled her into a searing kiss. It was as if they'd never done it before and would never get the chance again. But then he kissed her a second time and it was just as desperate. They were breathless for each other. Eager and panting and only catching a breath when things went white.

He couldn't let go, but he turned them far enough that he could kick the door shut. She had her hands on either side of his head, holding him steady for her lips. It was a different dance this time, full of noises and need, and she tasted wonderful, perfect. Damn it, he'd been starving for this. *This* with her fingers in his hair, and his arm around her back until they stumbled into the couch.

That didn't stop them. A clumsy elbow in his rib made her freeze. "I'm sorry. Are you all right—?"

He gathered her in his arms and drew her back to the couch. Then she pushed him until he either had to raise his legs or break them. He chose correctly because she straddled his waist. "I'm fine," he said. "You?"

"Perfect."

"Yes, you are." He pulled her straight down into another

kiss. It was long and deep, and her hands were on his chest, touching every part she could reach. He'd never wanted to be naked so badly, but he couldn't let go of her. Not yet.

She tweaked his nipple as her hand passed, making him arch high, with her thighs tightening around his hips. That made his cock impossibly harder.

She grinned against his mouth, and the kiss became slow and languid with tiny breaths and long moans. Her body rested on his so he could feel her heat and her pointed little nipples.

Then his stomach rumbled. So loudly he wanted to punch a wall. It made her laugh, but the moment—the swirling space they'd disappeared in—was gone.

"I didn't have a chance to eat much today, what with trying to get to your class. So it's your fault."

"Since I'm parched and starving, I'll take the blame."

She started to move away, but he stopped her. "No paperwork emergencies pending?"

She shook her head. "Ever since I got a new hole punch, the papers have been behaving themselves."

"Okay, then. We have time for food."

"Thanks, your highness," she said, and then she climbed off him.

While he went to the kitchen to check on his beverage selection, Lisa stayed in the living room with the old bookcase and super ugly chairs. The other night she hadn't seen much of the brownstone. Only his bedroom, really. But she was getting an eyeful now. He felt weird about the strange decor only when he had guests, and that almost never happened.

The oversize fridge was alarmingly bare. Luckily, there were some drinks. "I have bottled water…" he called. "…or there's Sapporo, Heineken, Blue Moon…"

"Whoa, this kitchen is huge." She pushed against him to take a peek. "That looks a lot like my fridge, except I also use mine for food. Actually, that's a lie. It looks nothing like my fridge. You could store half a cow in this ridiculous thing."

"It's a shame that I don't cook," he said. They were still bent over staring at the contents. "I've been told this is a true chef's paradise."

"Huh," she said as she wandered away. When he stood up, he found her checking out the six-burner gas stove and the stainless-steel sink.

"I think I told you how my uncle left the place to me? Well, if you're in need of pots, I'm your man." He gestured to the bevy of copper pots hanging over a sturdy oak island. "So, what's it going to be?"

"I'll have a Heineken, please. You must have been close to him."

"My uncle?" He grabbed two bottles. "When I was very young, yes. He had an open-cockpit airplane he doted over. Used to take me for rides. I loved it because he did a lot of stunts. Went to air shows all over the country."

"That sounds pretty awesome for a little kid."

He handed her the opened beer. "My brother, who wasn't a big fan of air travel, decided he wanted to go up. Probably because I was enjoying it so much. But he got sick all over himself and my uncle. That was it for plane rides."

They'd drifted back to the living room and the overabundance of aircraft memorabilia. "Both of you had to stop?"

He nodded. Took a swig of beer. "I got Uncle Frank's house because Warren was in line to get the family home. Frank was more interested in his planes than people, so no heirs. He was very wealthy. He's got patents on some aircraft parts that are still used in a lot of major airlines."

"Wow. When did you move in?"

"A little over four years ago. When I came back to New York after my residency in Baltimore."

"You'd already become a licensed physician."

He nodded.

She touched one of the small planes that dotted the decor. "Nice that you had this to come back to."

"I haven't done much with it. I was more interested in completing the fellowship at Mount Sinai initially. Then... well, the Center was left to both of us."

She turned to look at him, her brows drawn in a delicate frown. She looked absolutely beautiful in her leggings and pink top, strong and perfectly toned. "You mean you and—"

"Warren, yes. But wait. Food. You want to call in or go out?"

"I had sort of planned to eat naked...but sure, we can go out."

"We'll call in." He wanted to steal her away to his bedroom now. Let them die tragically from starvation in each other's arms. "Have I told you how great you were teaching that class?"

Smiling, she nodded. "Five or six times."

"That's because I mean it." He caught her hand and pulled her close. "Everyone loved it—"

"Too much. I have no idea why I said I'd consider doing another lesson. I'm not qualified to do more than what I did today."

He kissed her, slipping his fingers under the waistband of her leggings, her skin warm and soft. She curled up against his chest. Blindly they both set their bottles on the bookcase at the same time. Daniel moved his hand down until he reached the edge of her panties. God, just breathing her in—

Her stomach growled. It wasn't nearly as loud as his,

and he might have overlooked it if she hadn't broken the kiss and burst out laughing.

"All right, fine. The stomachs have spoken," he said, reluctant to let her go. After a peck on the tip of her nose, he led her to the kitchen drawer next to the range and took out a large stack of menus. "I've got pizza," he said, throwing the first menu on the counter. "Pasta and pizza, Thai, Chinese, Chinese, Chinese, Indian, burgers and cupcakes, American, sushi, vegetarian, deli, Mediterra—"

"Wait. Go back."

He picked up the last one.

"More."

"Can you give me a hint?"

"Fine. That first one. Pizza."

He grinned as he fished it out from the bottom of the stack.

"Which is your favorite?" she asked, looking at the front pictures.

"It doesn't matter," he said. "They don't make a pizza I don't like, so you pick."

She shook her head. "No, you're missing the point. You have, like, thirty menus, and this one was not only on top, it's a mess. So I figure this is the place you order from the most. And then I figured if that were true, you probably ordered the best pizza ever. So which one is it?"

"Well done, Sherlock," he said in an admittedly horrible British accent. Which he wouldn't do again. "Cheese. The kind where you bend it in half and burn the roof of your mouth."

"Sounds wonderful. Order, please? I'd do it, but they clearly know you."

He whipped out his phone, but when he hung up, she was back in the living room, looking at the books. "How long?"

"Twenty-five minutes." And he knew exactly how they'd spend the time.

He joined her, slinging an arm around her waist. He nuzzled her neck where it met her shoulder. "So, you must've been a detective," he said. "Back when you were a cop."

Her whole body tensed. He cursed himself up one side and down the other. He almost let her go, but she made the first move, slipping out of his embrace.

Shit. "I'm so sorry. I know you don't like to talk about it. My mistake. I hope I'll never make it again, but to be honest, I might."

"It's okay. It's not a big deal. Yes, I was a detective."

He went to her but didn't touch. Instead he stood very close. And she let him. "I truly am sorry."

"I know. It's fine. I promise." She kissed him, briefly, nothing heavy. Then nodded at the books. "Have you read all these?"

"Not even a sampling. Those are all Frank's books. I haven't had a lot of free time. Why do you think this place looks like something out of the Warner Brothers back lot?"

"Come on, it's interesting."

"No, it isn't. But I'll get around to making it my own at some point." He smiled, somehow not surprised she was okay with interesting over chic. "Come, I'll give you the rest of the tour."

THE PIZZA HAD been crazy good, and the cold beer had been the perfect touch. Between the two of them, they'd almost polished it off. She certainly felt better, even though they'd eaten in the huge dining room instead of bed. He'd shown her around the entire large house before they'd eaten, except for the only room she'd remembered.

His bedroom seemed different in the light of day. Again, the furnishings were weird but the linens they pulled down were as sleek and modern as the bed itself. The rest of the room wasn't. Uncle Frank really didn't have an eye for decorating.

Daniel grabbed several condoms and put them on his nightstand. They had one pillow each and far too many clothes on.

"You know what? I'm actually pretty tired after all that pizza."

His face! He looked as if she'd busted his favorite toy.

"Kidding," she said, walking around the bed to rest her head against his chest. "I hereby promise that until you have a proper orgasm, I won't make any more jokes, okay?"

"Okay," he said. "But can you let go of me now so we can get undressed?"

She tweaked his still-covered nipple. "Are we doing this fast, slow or sexy?"

"All of the above?"

"You do the slow and sexy parts. I'm stripping." She started with her T-back, whipping it off and tossing it over her shoulder.

"I like your idea better," Daniel said. He yanked his own T-shirt off and followed quickly with his track shorts.

"Ooh, nice jock," she said, cupping his cup.

"That's not a cup. That's my ridiculously manly cock."

She laughed as she pushed off her leggings. "Talk, talk, talk. That's all you ever want to do."

He was out of the jockstrap in record time. When she looked up, she realized he hadn't been kidding by much. The last two times had been whirlwinds. This time, well, they had time.

Naked and gorgeous, his chest rising and falling rapidly, he stepped closer. "You need help with that?"

Lisa had already slipped off her shoes and socks, but

her pink thong was still on. "Tear this and you die," she said, right before she bumped into him.

He hissed at the contact against his erection, but he had the wherewithal to lower her thong carefully until it fell to the floor, then pick her up caveman style and toss her onto the bed.

She squealed with surprise and then laughed. He kissed her as she was sitting up and she'd imagined this very scenario more than once. Them, on the big bed, wanting to please each other with lips and tongues and touch.

She was on her back as they took a breath break. Seconds later he straddled her, knees bent at the top of her thighs, arms stiff next to her shoulders. Mouth perfectly aligned.

"God, I could..." He was far enough away that they could look into each other's eyes.

"What's stopping you?"

"I have no idea," he whispered.

The kiss that followed was full of heat and passion and *want*. When they were both wrecked from kissing and touching, they were in the exact same position breathing each other's breath as if that was the only source of oxygen. He kissed her again, and it was even better than the last. Synchronized bliss.

Shifting to the left, he balanced himself so perfectly that his right hand was free to explore. It wasn't a very complicated trail. He cupped her breast, and with every breath they stole, he massaged her flesh and swirled his finger around her nipple. Then he ran his palm down her ribs, whispered his fingers across her tummy and ended the tour with his index finger on her clit.

"Oh, very good," she whispered, arching up to meet that talented finger. "Although, please calm down. You're not allowed to keel over from a heart attack."

"Don't worry about me," he said, nipping at her lower lip.

"Unless you're some kind of superathlete, you're not going to last long. Besides, I want to play with your penis."

His barked laugh was just enough to make him tumble to her side. "You make it sound like the two of you are going out to the swings together."

"Hmm. Sounds interesting, but I've got you here now, so I'm fine. More than fine." She turned on her side, and they each moved closer so more parts could touch. The kisses this time were sweeter. She loved the way he paid attention, how he repeated the things she liked while dropping or changing what she didn't. It boded very well for the future.

God, a future with Daniel. It would be short-lived, but exciting. Not just in the bedroom, but in every aspect. Talking to him, with his sense of humor and smarts, was a pleasure. Watching him be Dr. Cassidy, built of energy and compassion. She may not get a happily-ever-after, but who did? While she had him, Lisa was going to have a hell of a ride.

By the time she felt her orgasm take hold, she could no longer think. Her hand that had been steadily pumping and teasing him had dropped away. He squeezed her shoulders and pulled away at the worst possible time.

"Hey, not fair."

"Soon," he said as he slipped on a condom. "Missionary okay?"

"Any position's okay with me, as long as I get to see your face when you come."

"I want to watch you, too." He settled between her legs. They hadn't stopped staring at each other. "You are astonishingly beautiful…" He kissed her softly. "And so much more."

She arched again, unable to help herself. She knew he believed the words he'd just said, and she wondered if he would feel the same way if he knew the truth about her. "I want you inside me. Please. Now would be good."

His smile dimmed as his intensity built. Guiding himself, he pushed the head of his cock inside her. "Now would be damn good," he said, his voice a rumble of heat and desire. Then he thrust with his weight behind it, filling her.

She cried out, put her hands on the wood of his headboard. Good thing she had because he did it again, the thickness of his cock making her gasp. It felt amazing. Then he bent forward, and this time when he filled her, his cock rubbed straight over her clit. It was like the Fourth of July. "God, yes," she said, moving faster. "Daniel, please. I want...I..."

"What, you gorgeous creature? Anything at all. If you want it, I'll give it to you."

"This," she said, opening her eyes, when she hadn't even realized they'd been closed. "This. You. Us."

He brought them both to a shattering climax, her first, him seconds after.

But it couldn't erase the shock or the regret.

Of course she calmed down more quickly than he did, and then excused herself to visit the en suite. After turning on the water, she leaned on her palms, her eyes closed once more. She didn't dare look at herself yet. Not when she wanted so desperately to remember the sexy parts, the laughing, sharing a pizza. The innocent parts that didn't cause her chest to tighten. She wished she could turn back time. She would have stopped him from telling her those private things. About his uncle and his brother. And she sure as hell wouldn't have called them an *us*.

12

DANIEL LOOKED AT the empty side of his bed, wishing Lisa had stayed. He'd asked, she'd declined, and that was that. No apple this time, either. It would have been nice, though. His shower was big enough for two and then they'd have both been late for work.

After pulling on a pair of boxers, he went through his routine: shower, shave, coffee, *New York Times*. Normal, average, except that he kept noticing things. The brownstone *was* odd. While the kitchen was more suited to Gordon Ramsay and the shower was great, the rest of the place looked old and…sad.

He liked airplanes well enough, but jeez. It all fit his uncle to a T. Daniel should do something about it, see what this house would look like if it fit him. Honestly, he had no idea where he'd start. Eve would know a decorator. Right now, though, he needed to get a move on.

With his to-go cup in hand, he locked his front door and found Warren at the bottom of the steps. Fear stopped him in his tracks. His mother had died. "What's wrong?"

"What's wrong? You can start with the fact that you don't answer your phone. Or open a text. Is it just me you've blocked, or does that go for anyone from the life you've abandoned?"

He could breathe again. "I was told you'd be out of town."

"And now I'm back." Warren's lips pressed together until they'd paled while his neck and cheeks reddened.

Overall, he looked as perfectly put together as ever. Taller than Daniel by an inch, dressed like the clothes-horse he was. He could have been on the cover of *Forbes* any day of the week.

When his brother looked up again, he seemed calmer. "I called you four times last night. Dr. Elliot has to go to San Diego for a funeral. He's leaving tomorrow."

"I had company and I wasn't on call, so I turned off my cell."

Warren sighed. "Come on. I'll take you to the clinic and we can talk on the way."

Daniel nodded. Warren opened the door to the illegally double-parked town car and waited for Daniel to get in. He smiled to himself and almost jokingly assured Warren that he wouldn't make a run for it. But sadly, too much rancor had been festering between them.

When they were both seated, Daniel leaned forward to give the driver the address, but Warren stopped him.

"He already knows. Now sit back and listen. It's important that you take over Elliot's patients. If you still insist on pursuing this ridiculous quest to find your personal nirvana, I won't stop you. But I do demand you follow through with any patients you'll see in the next two days. You know what our patients expect."

"I know exactly what's expected of me, Warren. But it seems you don't give a damn that Dad had encouraged me to take time off."

"Three months? *Our* father wanted you to take three months off."

Daniel regretted his words although he wasn't going to apologize. His sabbatical wasn't the problem.

"I don't want to do this now," Warren said. "We need to speak privately, and not when we'll be late for work."

"You're right. We do need to talk. Because I'm not going to be the partner you expect."

"What does that even mean?"

Daniel shook his head. "I think we should hire another doctor after Elliot retires."

"You're replacing Elliot. You were always supposed to replace him." Warren's eyes narrowed to a glare. "Or have you forgotten?"

"And who's going to replace Dad?" Daniel asked quietly.

Warren blinked and turned to look out his window.

Neither of them spoke for a few blocks. Then Daniel said, "The point I was trying to make is that even with me, we need to think about hiring additional staff. The hours are brutal, but they don't have to be."

Warren leaned forward, but he was staring directly into Daniel's eyes. "Don't you dare start trying to change things at the Center. You haven't been there for months, leaving me to take care of everything. I don't give a good goddamn what kind of spiritual journey you're on. The profits from that business paid for you to have the best education in the world and a standard of living that's beyond most people's dreams. Was all that so you could work at a free clinic for no pay and not think twice about it? Go ahead, use your trust fund to live. To eat. To be a hero for a bunch of homeless people. It's all thanks to Dad and me, and you know what? I'm glad he's dead. That he can't see what you've become. He'd have died of the shame."

Daniel hadn't looked away. He should have, because Warren didn't know a thing about what was going on inside him because Warren had never asked. And when Daniel had tried to explain, right after their father died, his loving brother had told him he didn't give a shit. That their duty was to take their rightful place. Anything else was self-indulgent bullshit.

How tempting it had been to ask Warren what he knew about their father's plan to expand well beyond an additional doctor or two. Just to see the look of shock on his face. "I can see you've moved into Dad's footsteps without missing a trick. How many conferences have you gone to in the last four months? Did you miss Alan's birthday? Your anniversary?"

"Shut up, Daniel. You don't know anything about anything. So just go, would you?"

Daniel hadn't noticed the car had stopped. He stepped out, looked back at his brother. "I'll see you tomorrow."

"Fine. Shut the door. I have patients to see."

LISA HAD TO admit that she'd wondered if working at the clinic appealed to her because volunteering was rewarding or because she liked Daniel. As the second day without him at the clinic settled into an eerie re-creation of her three hours there yesterday, the answer was…actually not that clear.

She'd wager if she'd been assigned to intake again, or some other job where she could interact with people, she would've been happier. But as it was, digitizing patient files in the corner office was plain old boring.

Her cell buzzed and she started smiling even before she checked the incoming text. On the plus side, working in solitary gave her lots of privacy to read Daniel's messages. He'd been seeing patients at the Center for two days but he'd found lots of time to squeeze in texts. It was 4:30 and she'd already heard from him four times.

Chinese tonight? Or pizza again?

Lisa read between the lines and laughed out loud. He'd been a terrific sport. Indulging her new cheese-pizza addiction. They'd had it again last night at his place after a grueling day working with his brother. She'd made it up to him with two hours of sex, and that was after she'd given him a back massage.

Tonight she had a surprise for him. Well, two, actually.

Chinese. I'll pick it up. Let me know what time.

She set the phone aside and thought of the tote she'd stashed in her locker. Her shift ended in an hour, and while she would've had enough time to run to her apartment to grab a change of clothes, she didn't trust herself not to chicken out. The past two nights he'd asked her to stay over. Tonight she wouldn't disappoint him.

It would be a big step and it felt a little scary even now if she thought too much about it. Though last night had been the true test. While she knew tension existed between Daniel and his brother, after spending eleven hours at the Center, Daniel hadn't said a word about Warren. Most of his conversation was geared toward the cool technology the Center boasted. She'd listened but admittedly, his enthusiasm was all she cared about.

The divorce case for her real job was an ongoing snooze fest in the mornings. She was going through records, both public and personal. It was almost as exciting as data input here at the clinic. But at least she'd become something of an expert at filling in the medical codes and transcribing notes. That was the biggest challenge of her day. Doctors really did have horrible handwriting.

A quick look at the material she'd just entered made her moan. She'd had her fingers on the wrong keys, so everything was gibberish and she'd have to do it again. It wasn't totally her fault. Different keyboard than she was used to, basically a different language to learn.

Finally, she got the file entered correctly and was about to move to the next when there was a light knock. The door hadn't been shut, but she turned around, expecting Hector or one of the doctors. She hadn't expected Eve. Much less expected to find her smiling as she came in. Also, she was wearing a gorgeous outfit and she'd left her dark, shoulder-length hair down. She must've just come from the Center.

"How are you doing?"

"Fine." Lisa smiled. "And you?"

Eve glanced at the finished stack and then sat on one of the two blue velvet wing chairs. One of them had a patched rip in the back wing, but they were still the best chairs in the place. "Have a minute?"

Lisa wasn't going to say no. She saved everything on the computer, wondering if they fired volunteers.

"It must be strange not to have Daniel around," Eve said.

Lisa blinked. "Um, I guess." She'd been called to the principal's office a time or two in her day, and it felt exactly like this. Only she refused to squirm.

Eve smiled. "He's probably told you I've known him all his life. We're cousins, and after college, I went to work at the Center."

Lisa nodded and waited while Eve studied her for a long uncomfortable moment.

"I believe Daniel's the happiest he's been since high school. Academically and professionally speaking, of course he's been terrifically satisfied, but it's different now. I think you have something to do with that."

Lisa opened her mouth, but she hesitated when she met Eve's eyes. Something was troubling her, and Lisa didn't want to interrupt.

"As much as Daniel loves working at the clinic, he has another obligation."

Lisa nodded. "The Center."

"It's where he belongs. Not that he doesn't belong here, but his skills as a neurologist are more than impressive. He was chief resident at Johns Hopkins. That's the equivalent of being valedictorian at Harvard. Every major hospital and private practice in the field wanted him to work with them. But I suppose everyone knew he'd end up with his father and Warren."

"He hasn't really talked about his school years. I didn't realize— I mean, I can see he's brilliant, but that's truly impressive."

"He has a gift. He's blossomed as a person here, but he's too good to be diagnosing yet another cold."

She was right. But only if being at the Center was something he wanted, which was none of Lisa's business. "Why are you telling me this?"

"When you first started here, I figured you were just another woman who had heard or read about Daniel. I imagine you're aware that there are women—smart, attractive women—who specifically search out certain types of medical professionals. The ones who can earn the big bucks. It's easy to think he'd be the perfect husband and father. He's great-looking, nice, funny. But he doesn't want that kind of woman. That's one of the reasons he hasn't been with anyone for almost two years."

Lisa's back straightened. "I did not come here because

of Daniel." Though technically that wasn't true, it was accurate in this discussion.

"I believe you. I don't think you're that at all. He's so proud of you he could burst. You know, he called me the night after the incident with the junkie. Actually, we're all proud and grateful. The point is, he couldn't say enough good things about you, and he hasn't done that in…well, since his first girlfriend in high school."

"I was glad to help." Lisa felt a little more relaxed, but she wasn't about to let down her guard. Eve was protective toward Daniel. Lisa had no doubt she would fight to the finish if she thought anyone was out to hurt her boy.

Eve narrowed her eyes. "I'm thinking ex-military?"

Ah. So this was an interrogation. "Something like that." This time Eve had to have noticed the chill in her tone.

"Never mind. Sometimes I'm too curious for my own good. He told me about how you handled the self-defense class, as well. I think it's wonderful, and so do all the women who were there."

"Good. I hope they'll all follow up with a certified class."

"I'm actually sorry I missed it."

Lisa smiled, still not quite understanding what was going on.

Maybe Eve saw the confusion in her expression, or maybe she just decided to spit it all out, but she leaned forward and lowered her voice. "I like how he is with you, Lisa. There's so much more life to him when he speaks of you. I don't want to meddle any more than I already have, but I did want to say that I understand what he sees in you. The truth is he needs to take his place alongside Warren. We'll miss him here at the clinic, but we'll find someone else to help out. Someone who won't be healing world leaders. If you can help him see that's where he belongs, wonderful. But he can't stay here for you. Nothing personal. I really do like and admire you. I think you're good for him."

"But if I steer him away from his destiny, I'm toast?"

"Something like that. Although not nearly as dramatic."

"Wait, is this your version of giving us your blessing?"

Eve laughed. Nothing shy about it, either. She was awfully personable when she wasn't scaring the hell out of someone.

"Well, I think you should know Daniel and I are just… friends." Lisa hated that she had trouble getting out the word and feeling as if she was somehow being a traitor for wanting to downplay their relationship.

"Whatever you're doing, it looks good on you both." Eve stood. "Now, I'd better get moving. The clinic is closing in fifteen minutes."

"For the record, this is right up there as one of the strangest conversations I've ever had."

Eve smiled. "Depending on how long your *friendship* with Daniel lasts, you and I will have at least a few more."

Great. Now there was another person who was going to hate her, or worse, if they learned that she'd been investigating Daniel for one of those aforementioned women, then topped it off by keeping him for herself.

Damn it, she had no one to blame for this mess but herself. She should have left the day Heather told her to forget about investigating Daniel. Hell, she'd had no reason to show up here in the first place. If she'd done her job properly, she'd have never learned that Daniel was wealthy enough right this minute to satisfy Heather's wildest dreams. That he would eventually leave the clinic for a highly successful career as a neurologist in a thriving practice.

The thought had bothered her lately, but usually she ignored it. Eve's little talk had brought new life to the problem. All Lisa could do was remind herself that Heather had paid for the minimum.

Shortly after Eve left, Lisa shut the computer off and left the files neatly stacked for, with any luck, someone else. Halfway down the hallway she received a call from her brother. She answered, but Logan's voice broke up terribly. "I'll call you back in a minute," she said. "Can't hear you."

Waiting for a reply, she made her way to the lounge. After grabbing her purse and tote, she went outside and called him back. "What's up?"

"I have a job for you. Tomorrow night I want you dressed to kill and at the NoMad Bar by 7:00. You asked to step up. Here's your chance."

"Playing dress-up wasn't what I had in mind."

"It's the job that's needed now. No picking and choosing."

"Right. What else?"

"I'll fill you in later. Now go find something classy to wear. Go for a designer name, elegant but a little revealing. Rent the Runway should have something. Go all out. You're meant to be noticed. Got it?"

"Yes. Absolutely." So much for seeing Daniel tomorrow...

"I have to go. Jesus, I'm late. Tomorrow."

"'Bye," she said to no one. She'd done the gown-rental thing several times and they'd always come through for her. Her phone rang again but it was a text from Daniel. He wanted to meet at his place in two hours.

She'd be late, depending on how long it took her to find a dress. Well, she was the one who wanted meatier cases. And it was good to shift her focus. Even if she and Daniel had a thing, soon he'd be diving headfirst into work at the Center.

Before texting him back, she trudged halfway to the

station, her thoughts traveling faster than her feet. Her conversation with Eve clarified something Lisa had already known. Soon, Lisa Pine was going to have to explain herself. She wasn't going to disappear, even though that would be a million times easier. It wouldn't be fair. The question was, when?

13

THE NOMAD BAR wasn't somewhere Lisa would have ever come on her own, and she couldn't imagine Daniel there. This place had that mix of being so expensive it eliminated the riffraff, and hipster quirky, which attracted the younger set. She had a seat at the left-hand corner of the bar, which clearly hadn't been made for women wearing tight dresses. After a few tries she finally found a position where she wasn't flashing the room.

It looked as if it was going to be a long night. Good thing she wasn't footing the bill for her vodka martinis. So far she'd had only one, and it was yummy, no doubt about it. But at twenty dollars a pop, come on.

She smiled at the bartender and then glanced around the room, careful not to linger on Logan sitting at a table in the far corner with a redhead Lisa didn't know. The woman could be a friend of his, or she could be CIA. Lisa was thinking the latter. She tried not to yawn. It would be bad for her seductress image.

The deal was to try to catch the attention of Mr. Travis King, a guest at the hotel and sleazeball sex trafficker. If she netted him, she was to play hard to get without becoming inebriated. It was imperative she stayed alert. And not let her mind wander to Daniel as she'd already done too many times. King and his friends had a reputation for drugging companions, then flying them out of the country and selling them for very high prices.

The magic hour was 9:30 and it couldn't come fast enough. If King didn't show up by then, it meant he'd be headed for his private jet and Lisa's part in the sting would be over for the night.

She refused to think about Daniel again. She'd see him soon enough. They had plans to meet at a restaurant around the corner. In the meantime, there were instructions that had to be followed to the letter, that needed to be performed seamlessly. If King did come through and take the bait, she wasn't to touch any food he ordered. If he bought her a cocktail, she would only pretend to drink it.

From seven to nine she was hit on six times. She'd had water served in a martini glass twice, which made her feel like a kid playing dress-up. But finally she received a text from Logan that she could leave. King never walked through, and now it was confirmed he was en route to the airport.

If she had her way, she'd take off this outfit straightaway, never to be worn again. The dress was beautiful, expensive, the neckline a lot lower than she would've liked. Her style was generally a lot more conservative. Unfortunately, she might have to repeat her role in a couple of nights.

Just as she slid off the stool her phone rang. Daniel texted with a change of plans. Could she meet him at the clinic?

At least it was after hours and no one but Daniel would be there…

AFTER HIS LAST scheduled day at the Center, Daniel had gone straight to the clinic to help with the evening shift. Not completely out of altruism. Lisa had some work thing

she was doing and wouldn't be free until around 10:00.
While it felt good to be back, the fit wasn't quite as comfortable as it had been. Probably had a lot to do with seeing
three patients in a row who wanted antibiotics for a cold.

One of the volunteer GPs, Carol White, had asked him
for a consult about her patient. He'd taken over the case,
and at 9:30 Daniel knew he wouldn't be going anywhere
until they'd found a way to treat Javier Moreno. In a few
minutes, Lisa would be there. He should've canceled. Told
her to reroute her taxi home.

Better yet, to his place. But when he got his cell phone
out, he couldn't do it. Selfishly, he wanted to see her. Even
if it was just for a few minutes. Last night she'd stayed over
for the first time, and he was hoping for a repeat. Waking
up next to her had lit up his day.

With no small amount of effort, he shoved aside thoughts
of her and glanced at his initial notes again. Javier was still
on the gurney, talking to Eve. He wanted to go home even
though he'd had a seizure and he'd stumbled with dizzi-
ness when he'd had his X-ray.

Javier and his family had been coming to the clinic for
a couple of years. He'd come in tonight after work because
his headaches had worsened throughout the day.

"We just want to make sure you'll be okay getting home,"
Eve said. "Dr. Cassidy is monitoring your vitals, making
sure you don't have any more seizures."

"I'm grateful and everything, but I don't like to be gone
so much at night. Gloria's mom left at seven."

"Tell you what," Eve said, putting her hand on his shoulder. "I'll give the kids a call, tell them what's going on, and
ask if they need anything."

"I can—" He tried to sit up, but fell back on the gurney.
"Just give me a minute. I'll be okay."

"I'll ask someone to bring you some juice. That should help."

Eve smiled as she left him, but she lost the grin as soon as she turned her back. Daniel walked with her to the lounge. Two nurses had stayed late. Luckily, one of them, probably Beverly, had just made a fresh pot of coffee.

"I think you're right," Eve said, handing him a cup and then pouring a coffee for herself. "We've seen this before."

Daniel nodded. "We should start our calls with Sloan-Kettering and Mount Sinai Roosevelt. They'll have the equipment to handle this."

"Dr. Cassidy," she said, in a very different tone of voice. "It looks as though you have some special company."

Behind him, Beverly filled the room with a startlingly shrill wolf whistle. When Daniel turned around, he understood. He set his coffee on the fridge.

"I had a thing," Lisa said, her free hand tugging at the neckline of a striking red dress that ended a few inches above her knees.

Daniel struggled not to sweep her into his arms. "You look like a…"

"High-class hooker?"

"A damn movie star," he said. His gaze went to her silver stiletto heels and kept rising. He knew her legs were stunning, but in those heels? Jesus, he wanted to take her to exam room 3 right that minute. Hike up that dress—

"Lisa, if I looked like you, I would not be blushing," Beverly said with a shake of her head.

Daniel cleared his throat as he met Lisa's eyes. "Come with me a minute?"

Lisa nodded, placed a hand at her neckline.

"Be careful, Dr. Dan," Beverly added as she wiggled her eyebrows. "You know firsthand what she can do."

"Okay, you're to call me Dr. Cassidy and no more whistling in the clinic."

The nurse tried to hide her grin. "Yes, Dr. Cassidy."

He wasn't actually bothered, and he knew that since the self-protection extravaganza, his days of being an aloof and revered doctor were over. "Good. And if you made the coffee, thanks."

He and Lisa met at the door, and just as he locked onto her gaze, Eve said, "You look beautiful, Lisa." Then to Daniel, "I'll go make those calls and hope for the best."

LISA WAITED UNTIL she and Daniel were in an empty exam room before she said, "I really thought everyone else would have gone home by now. I actually have something to change into that doesn't scream 'hooker.'"

"You look gorgeous, but that's not why I brought you in here. Which is a pity. Maybe another time we can… What am I saying." He shook his head. "There's been a complication," he said. "About which I will tell you all I can as soon as we finish kissing."

He had his hands on her waist, and at the touch of his lips, she relaxed for the first time in what felt like weeks. Putting her arms around his neck was as natural as breathing, and kissing reminded her again of all the ways the two of them could make each other feel good.

He ran his hands up her back, pushed his hips against her, letting her feel the beginning of his erection. A few seconds later, he stepped back until they were no longer touching. "I'm sorry. I want…so very much. But I've got a patient."

"Oh." She saw the concern in his eyes. He looked tired. "Do you want me to leave?"

"Not really. But it's likely I'll be here for a couple more hours, at least."

"I'll stick around. If you think I can be of help."

He sighed. "Anytime you want to leave, tell me. I'll make sure you get a cab. In fact, I'll just give you the keys to my place."

She kissed him again. "How do you know I won't walk away with all the silver?"

He moved away just far enough to mumble, "You were a police officer."

"I'm not anymore."

His fingertips skimmed her cheek, then down to her jaw. She'd closed her eyes to let the feel of him wash over her. A very soft kiss landed on the tip of her nose.

"I hope you kept the handcuffs," he whispered.

"Go." She was the one to step back this time. She'd needed to before things got out of hand. "Don't worry about me."

"I have to wait for Eve to make the calls."

"Can you tell me about the patient?"

He shook his head. "I'm his doctor."

"Right. Patient confidentiality."

"You could talk to Eve, though. Since we might need you to help out if things get tricky."

She had no idea what he meant by that, only that it sounded ominous. "I'll get changed, grab a cup of coffee and find her."

He kissed her one more time, another quick peck. "Thanks."

EVE WAS IN the office where they'd had their talk yesterday. She'd just disconnected a call when she saw Lisa. "Come on in."

Lisa sat in one of the wing chairs, having changed from the red dress into a white boho-chic peasant dress she'd picked up from a street vendor. Oh, God, how great her sandals felt after ditching the six-inch heels she'd been wearing. "Sorry about that outfit."

"If I could look as good as you do, I'd never wear anything else."

Lisa laughed at the blatant lie. "Daniel mentioned a problem patient."

Eve got serious. "Javier. He's a janitor at Chamberlain High School. Daniel thinks he might have a skull-base brain tumor. We can't treat him here, and I've been calling hospitals to see if we can get help, but it's not easy."

"Why, because he doesn't have insurance?"

"Partly. Mostly because if Daniel's right, which I'm sure he is, the prognosis isn't very good. It's very difficult to see those kinds of tumors, let alone remove them. Some hospitals have a full slate of patients without insurance, and some don't have the equipment or the staff to help."

"What can I do?"

Eve looked exhausted. "Keep the coffeepot full. Check in with Dr. Carol's nurse, see if there are any more latecomers that need anything. Mostly, though, you can check in with Daniel. Give him a smile."

"I'm on it."

IT WAS ALMOST 11:00 when Daniel gave up. Not on Javier, but on finding a hospital in the greater New York area who could give him the care he needed. There was only one place left. He wasn't sure why it was so difficult to move forward. He owned 50 percent of Madison Avenue Neurological Center. But at the moment, Warren was running things and out of respect, Daniel wouldn't simply waltz in with Javier. Particularly since he knew the Center was close to capacity.

He was sure of his diagnosis and certain that it would be a difficult and costly pro bono case. But it offered Javier the best chance he'd have for survival. That wasn't something Daniel was willing to ignore. So he hoped he and Warren could put their personal differences aside. The few times they'd seen each other the past two days, they'd interacted reasonably well.

Lisa was helping clean up the lounge, looking cool and sweet in her hippy dress. It made him smile, though, to see her so comfortable doing whatever needed to be done. The moment he'd seen her his spirits had lifted. But he was glad she was busy, because he needed to make this call in private. Except for Eve, of course.

She'd suggested he call over an hour ago, but he'd needed to be sure. The hour wouldn't have hurt Javier's chances, but it definitely gave Daniel the time he'd needed to develop his case. Now he was ready to put it out there. Warren could say no. There was no familial bond that would sway him one way or another, but he might do it for Eve. His father had, from time to time, helped the clinic's patients. Daniel needed to remember those things, remember that his dad hadn't always been wrapped up in his own ego.

"I can say you don't even know I'm calling, if you want." Eve had given him the desk. She was leaning against the credenza, looking as if she was ready to leap at the word she was needed. Hell, she was always ready to do that.

"I'll take care of it. But thank you." He dialed Warren's cell.

"Isn't it a little late to be calling?" Warren said, after picking up on the second ring. "Or was I a misdial?"

"Not a mistake, and yes, it's late. I have a patient here at the clinic who needs a lot more help than I can give him."

Warren stayed quiet during the entire presentation. And for a long time after. Daniel prepared himself for the worst. Then, "Fine. We can find an available bed. But you'll be responsible for his care. Including finding a surgeon and an-

esthesiologist who are willing to do this pro bono. I'll cover
the admin costs. You're also responsible for the ambulance.
I'll let the night team know you're coming. They'll meet
you in the bay. Document everything. We haven't had a
skull-base tumor in a while. Everyone can use a brush-up."

The relief rolling through Daniel almost made him high,
although that was probably just the lack of sleep. He and
Lisa had been up until 1:30 in the morning. "Thank you,
Warren."

"You're welcome," he said and paused. "Oh, hell, if you
have trouble finding a surgeon, I'll look at rearranging my
schedule."

Daniel knew his brother had disconnected but he couldn't
seem to move. He was too stunned to do anything but give
Eve the nod. Raw with the unexpected swell of emotion, he
lowered his phone. Clearly he'd underestimated his brother.

Eve hadn't—she'd already called the private ambulance
company they used. "They'll be here in twenty. Now we
have to get Javier to agree to go."

"He will." Daniel finally started to gather his wits. He
didn't have to tell her about Warren's offer—he had a feeling it wouldn't be a surprise. It seemed she knew his brother
better than he did. "Javier will do whatever it takes to make
sure he's here for his family," Daniel said as they started
down the hall.

She slowed a little. "Let me tell him the news. You go
find Lisa, explain what's going on."

"Yeah, I should send her on home."

"I didn't say that, Daniel. In fact, I think you should
take her along. Let her see the Center. I think she'd learn
a lot about you and what you're going through if she saw
the other side of the equation."

Daniel let Eve walk ahead as he thought about what
she'd said, but just before she reached exam room 2, he

called out, "You go home right after we get Javier squared away."

Eve, who never listened to anybody, nodded.

SINCE ARRIVING NINETY minutes ago, Lisa had been entertaining herself in the very upscale visitors' lounge while Daniel was busy with Mr. Moreno. The couch was the most comfortable thing she'd ever sat on. The free beverage station had better coffee, Earl Grey tea and hot chocolate than any coffeehouse she'd been to. Even the magazines were way out of her price range. Not only had she never heard of these mags, *Dolce Vita* cost almost thirty-eight bucks an issue, *Upscale Living* went for fifty dollars, and the crème-de-la-crème magazine for the rich was *The Robb Report* at $108.88. It was mind-boggling. And also, why the $8.88? Was that a supersecret sign that only billionaires recognized?

She'd been around the block a couple of times, considering she'd been a cop in Manhattan, but this place was making her feel like a hick from Hicksville. It must cost a fortune to come to the Center.

A tall man who looked a lot like Daniel, only with less hair and glasses, walked into the lounge. "Hello. I'm Warren Cassidy. You're a friend of Daniel's, Lisa…?"

She rose to her feet, tried to say Pine, but she couldn't. Physically couldn't. Finally extending her hand, she said, "That's right. I met him where I volunteer."

"Please, don't get up on my account. You must like it then, to keep volunteering."

"I do," she said, taking a seat again. "Very much. The staff is wonderful and friendly, and more often than not, the patients are fascinating. Although I don't see too many. Usually I'm away filing or working on data entry." God, the way she was chattering. They had to quit sticking her alone in the back.

There was nothing about his demeanor or his expression that made her think he knew about her personal relationship with Daniel, yet somehow...

"Daniel seems to like it there, as well."

"He does a lot of good. And he's nice. He makes people feel comfortable."

"I see. He hasn't told me much about his work, but I assume he's helped a great many people, given his gift for medicine."

"Neurology, in particular, from what I hear."

Warren smiled, and that was where the similarity ended. Daniel's smile was warm and genuine. Warren needed to keep working on it. Or maybe she wasn't seeing him at his best. "He's mentioned the Center?"

"Many times. So has Eve."

"Then you know that Daniel is an exceptional physician. We're hoping he can stand to tear himself away to come back to his roots. But now I realize there are many reasons for him to stay where he is."

Lisa stiffened her spine and held his gaze. "What are you implying?"

"That there seems to be a lot to recommend working to help those who are less fortunate or disenfranchised."

"It's fulfilling," she said. He was Daniel's brother, so she'd be nice and not assume he was being a jerk. "Everyone deserves some help now and then. And when they're not made to feel like failures or lesser beings, they tend to give back to their community. A win-win situation. But I'm sure Eve has told you that already."

His smile seemed a little warmer. "Please avail yourself of all the amenities. In that cabinet—" he nodded toward a stunning piece of furniture she'd seen but hadn't investigated "—there are blankets and pillows. It was very nice to meet you."

She stood up and held her hand out to him again. "You as well, Dr. Cassidy."

He disappeared down a hall, and she had to wonder what Daniel had said about her.

Another twenty minutes went by, and while she'd meant to get a blanket and a pillow, she hadn't. Instead, she stared at the painting on the wall. It was very soothing, that painting. It helped her think instead of jumping to conclusions and making up stories when she didn't know the truth. She'd been predisposed to dislike Warren. He upset Daniel and she was definitely wearing Daniel goggles most of the time.

Warren might be the worst brother in the world. Or he could be genuinely on Daniel's side. Conclusion? She hated that she wanted to know which was true. But she'd made sure that she and Daniel didn't have that kind of relationship.

Then he walked into the room, and everything else fell away. "Hey, you're still awake. I don't remember if I told you about all the stuff in here."

"I'm good," she said. "What about you?"

He took a long look at her while sporting a small smile. She would have thought he meant to cause some mischief if they hadn't been on sacred ground. "You feel like going for a short walk?"

She got up, which was a yes, but she also nodded. "Where to?"

"The first floor." He held his hand out and she accepted it without hesitation. Being close to him for a short elevator ride felt good. Then he took her to a big room that had a lot of warnings on the door. She didn't bother to read them because Daniel would never take her anywhere unsafe. He held the door for her, and she stepped inside.

"Holy… This is like being on the starship *Enterprise*. Seriously," she said. "Did you just beam me up?"

He walked in back of her and then drew her against his front. "I'll beam you up later, promise, but now I want to show you some modern miracles."

He steered her to a very long, uncomfortable-looking bed. It wasn't the strangest thing in the room by far. That honor was taken by a huge machine that looked like a giant electric mouth.

"This is a state-of-the-art catheterization lab. And this beauty is the Cath Unit. It helps us see crisp, distortion-free visualizations of the tiniest details, like blood vessels in the brain."

"It looks terrifying."

"Yes, but it's a miracle maker. Come on, there's something else." He led her to another room, which had a huge monitor. He did something and the screen showed a picture of a skull.

"This is a 3-D imaging computer simulation. It lets us see exactly where in the brain a tumor or embolism is located. When we have our plan of attack ready, we use a robotic arm to actually do the surgery."

"You have a robot?"

"There's a surgeon running the robot. So much about the ways we treat the brain has changed in just the last twenty years, it's astonishing. There are hundreds of people walking around today who had no chance of survival even five years ago."

She leaned back against the only piece of equipment in the room she knew she couldn't break: the wall. "This is amazing. You're amazing. Do you know that you light up when you talk about it?"

"Light up, huh? I thought that only happened when I saw you."

She smiled, knowing that he would come back to work here full-time sooner rather than later. The clinic was nice, but it wasn't *this*. And she was certain that if Heather had known what Lisa knew now, she'd have thought she'd died and gone to rich-husband heaven.

But Lisa wasn't going to think about Heather or anyone else but Daniel. He showed her all kinds of astonishing technology, and told her a bunch of stuff she didn't understand, but she didn't care. He was in his element. Only someone very special could be with a man like Daniel Cassidy.

And that certainly wasn't Lisa Pine.

14

LISA TOOK A big sip of coffee and turned back to her laptop screen. It was Saturday. The clinic was open today but they had enough volunteers on weekends and she was in serious need of catching up on her stupid divorce cases. She jumped when her cell phone rang. "What are you doing calling so early?"

"It's 11:30." Daniel paused. "Did I wake you?"

"No, but you should be asleep. What time did you end up leaving the Center?"

"You don't want to know." He sighed. "Hey, I'm sorry about last night. I should've known better than to drag you—"

"Stop it. You didn't drag me anywhere." She stifled a yawn, sneaked in another quick sip. "I'm glad I went. Your center is awesome, and I mean that in the most literal way."

"Were you glad to sleep in your own bed for a change?" he asked, his voice dipping lower.

"Um, you haven't seen my bed, or you wouldn't ask." Technically she'd spent only one night at his place, but yeah, she would've preferred staying there. But only with him. And he was busy with Javier. She hadn't wanted to distract him, so she'd taken a taxi to her apartment around 1:30. "How's Javier?"

"Things are looking good" was all he said, though she didn't think she'd done anything wrong by asking. "Where are you?"

"Home. Guzzling caffeine. Working. I got quite a bit done this morning, considering."

"Good. Can you get away for a little bit?"

"Daniel, I'm serious about you getting some sleep." She knew for a fact he hadn't had enough rest all week. But then, neither had she.

"I will. Later. Let's go get coffee."

She glanced at her laptop screen. Of course she should say no. She was tired and busy. He had to be exhausted. "Where?"

"HAVE YOU BEEN here before?" Daniel asked, holding her hand as they walked into the memorial park on a beautiful path that led to a row of cherry trees. Green-Wood Park was a popular place for locals and tourists alike.

"You'd think I would have, since it's the most beautiful place in Brooklyn, but no."

It felt weird holding hands with him, and she kept looking around for anyone who knew her real name, but when Daniel smiled at her as if she'd brought the sunshine, she relaxed.

"Come on…" She tugged on his hand. "You said you'd tell me how much sleep you got."

He led her down another wide pathway. "Maybe three hours. There were a lot of tests to be run and decisions to be made."

Only three? She'd make sure he did something about that. "Earlier when I asked about Javier, I wasn't asking you to break confidentiality."

"I know." Daniel squeezed her hand and brought it to his lips for a quick kiss. It startled her, but she didn't tense. Didn't even look around. "I would've told you more on the phone but I was anxious to see you in person. Javier regards you as part of the team, by the way. He has no problem with anything I tell you."

She smiled. "All I do is make coffee."

"You also make his doctor very happy," he said, and she swallowed at the tender way he looked into her eyes. "We've imaged his brain from every possible angle. Two other doctors have reviewed his case, and we're all in agreement that we shouldn't wait to operate. At least, that's the latest word. We haven't technically gotten permission from Javier yet."

"He must be so worried."

"It's a scary thing, but he's lucky. He's got the best doctors in the country in his corner."

"So I've heard."

"I hope this isn't screwing up your whole day," he said.

She wondered if he was changing the topic on purpose or if his lack of sleep was to blame. "Nope. It's all good. God, it really is beautiful." She glanced around at the old trees and new greenery. "I've said that twice and we've barely seen anything. I feel like we're in a different country, let alone another borough."

"I've only been here once before, but I never forgot the experience."

"You probably should have slept instead." She moved closer to him until their shoulders touched.

"Maybe you're right, but this is where I wanted to be, and you're who I wanted with me. Everything about this place makes me calmer. The statues, the trees. The quiet."

She pulled him into a full-contact hug. There were other people in the huge park, so it didn't last as long as she wanted, but that was okay. When they moved on, neither one of them said much, soaking in the sounds of the wind ruffling the leaves and the birds chattering away.

"Are you going back tonight?" Lisa was a little sorry for breaking the silence.

He shook his head. "I'm banned until I get some solid rest. Things won't get hopping until tomorrow afternoon. Then I'll be busy for a couple of days. Eve's already found someone to cover for me at Moss Street."

They paused to look at a huge statue of an angel. They'd crossed into the cemetery, which was as beautiful and fascinating as anything the park had to offer.

Lisa really should have come before now. Everywhere she turned there was something gorgeous. The sculptures were as good as any she'd seen, the manicured lawns had breathtaking scope, and the mausoleums were works of art.

"I'm reasonably certain we'll be able to operate the day after tomorrow. That's when Dr. Hastings is available, and she's had more experience removing this type of tumor than almost anyone in the States." Daniel took yet another path, this time heading in the direction of a surprisingly large lake.

"She'll be set up next to Javier—remember I showed you? Using the console to see and direct the robotic arm. I'll be observing, and so will a number of other surgeons. Including Warren." He cleared his throat, his gaze directed at something in the distance. "I don't think I told you… Last night, when we arranged to transfer Javier to the Center, Warren offered to do the surgery pro bono if I couldn't find another surgeon."

"Wow." Her esteem for the man rose several notches. "That was very generous of him."

Daniel smiled at her. "It's okay to be surprised. I was, too. But Dr. Hastings is a great surgeon for this procedure."

They walked off the path down a long row of gravestones and statuary, taking time so she could read the carved names. When he stopped beneath the shade of a very old, very beautiful oak, she said, "That's…"

"My father's grave. He bought this plot when I was just a kid."

"It's beautiful."

He nodded. "I haven't been here since the funeral. Not sure why. Although, I never saw the point in talking to a slab of granite and a box of bones."

His hand tightened around hers. Not enough to hurt, but close.

"Actually, Dad bought two plots. The one beside him was supposed to be for my mom. Obviously that was before they divorced and she took off to Europe." Daniel's gaze stayed on the gravestone. "I blamed her. I was in my teens and I thought she was the most selfish woman on earth. Here was my dad, this brilliant, gifted doctor who'd devoted his life to healing people. Really important people. His waiting list wasn't just long—it was the who's who of Capitol Hill and dignitaries from across the globe.

"I wrote my mom this long email reminding her that she knew who he was when she married him and maybe that's why she even married him, for the fame and money, and how could she be so self-centered. His wife and kids needed to understand that medicine came first, that it should always come first. It was our duty to put up with hardly getting to see him. I got it in my head that we weren't so much a family as…I don't know…support staff."

Sighing, Daniel looked at Lisa with sad eyes. "You know that I never resented it when he missed birthdays or other holidays. I assumed that was Mom's job. I swear, odd as it sounds, it never occurred to me that there was a choice, that family and his career could be equally important."

"No, it doesn't sound odd," she said. "We believe the world we've been living in is the only one. It takes something major to see without the blinders of habit and years."

"You're right. I suspect that my obsessive learning had something to do with how long it took me to see. Thankfully, I never did send the damn email to my mother. She was right to leave. I think the only reason she hung around as long as she did was for Warren and me.

"She knew Dad. Obviously better than I did. Medicine was never supposed to be about fame. God, I was so naive. As far as his ego..." He smiled a little, shrugged. "I don't know many physicians who don't have big egos. Hell, we're human. But the healing came first. I lived my whole life with that as my prime directive." His voice trailed off and he took a deep breath. "I hadn't even planned on taking time off after my fellowship. I wanted to start at the Center the next day. Then I had that meeting with my dad."

Lisa wondered if he realized he was rubbing the top of his father's headstone. She doubted it. Part of her wanted to stop him, to turn her ankle or something so he wouldn't go on telling her his secrets. But the bigger part of her wanted him to continue. To get it all out. She'd deal with the consequences later.

"I thought we were going to discuss which patients I would take over, how to make the transition run smoothly after Dr. Elliot retired, that sort of thing. But Dad, all he wanted to talk about was expanding the Center, with both his sons in practice under him.

"He wanted his name on the biggest and best neurological center in the country." Daniel shook his head. "He was obsessed with it. Not the good he could do, but the accolades it would bring." He huffed a sorry laugh. "That was the only legacy he cared about. I couldn't even get him to change the subject. When I asked him what Warren thought about it, he said my brother didn't know anything yet—no one did.

"He must've seen my shock or disappointment because he told me to take some time to think it over. That for now, it was just between the two of us. It was like a falling dream, the kind where you wake up before you crash, but I couldn't wake up. For the first time in my life I wondered why he'd even had children. For bragging rights? Living tributes to him?"

He looked at Lisa again and she held her breath. She had no idea what to say or how to help. Or if he expected anything from her. She wanted to hug him again, but something held her back.

"Three days later he died in his office at the Center. A massive heart attack at sixty-four. He hadn't even been monitoring his own health." Daniel briefly closed his eyes. "What's most confusing? That I still want to be like him. I shouldn't. But he was the greatest doctor I've ever known. And he was also a terrible father and a worse husband. At his funeral, no one except the pastor said a word about the family."

Daniel turned back to the gravestone. "He did a lot of good. And I've always idolized him, but I don't want to miss out on my own life. I want to get married and have kids, and I want to really be with them. But I don't stand a chance unless I can let him go. Damn it, his shadow is long. I still can't see past it. But at least I know I have a choice."

Lisa shivered, and even though the day was warm, she hugged herself. Now that she could shift her gaze to anything but Daniel, she almost wept at the inscription on the grave. *Randall Cassidy.* Under that, a caduceus. And under that: *His legacy will live on.*

Daniel finally backed away and gave her a faint smile. "So now you know why I've been reluctant to go to the

Center. I needed time to think, and I felt alone. But going there this last week has been amazing. We have so many ways to bring hope to people, to save lives. I can see now that I'm needed there. Even more than at the clinic."

"Have you told anyone about the meeting with your father?"

He shook his head. "Only you."

Lisa touched his arm. She wanted to hold Daniel forever. Tell him that he was already walking his own road. He was more than just an exceptional doctor. He was a good man.

It felt like the worst selfishness to even think about how she couldn't let him go, even as she knew she couldn't hide the truth from him any longer. All she could do was hope he might still care for her after he knew who she really was.

"THANK YOU FOR TODAY. For listening," Daniel said as they neared the exit. He was sorry to reenter the real world. The traffic noises that crept into the park had helped ease their transition, but now there was no question they were in Brooklyn.

Lisa smiled as they came to a halt. "So you're going home to sleep now?"

He should. Damn, he really should. "You're probably busy."

She shrugged and he realized he hadn't noticed that her gray T-shirt tended to slip down her shoulder. And it was short enough that if she lifted her arms, he'd see skin above her tight black jeans. The damn pattern on the front of her shirt hid whether she'd gone braless.

"You want me to tuck you in?"

He was nodding before he actually heard what she'd said. "No, I don't want that. But if you were planning on staying home anyway…"

"Ah, you want to come to my place, get into my stupidly small bed and sleep while I work?"

"If that's okay with you…"

She didn't seem to share his enthusiasm. Instead of looking at him, her eyes were downcast and her grip had loosened.

"You know what?" he said. "I've already taken up more of your day than I should—"

"Stop. Yes. I'd like you to sleep while I do my thing. And maybe when you get up—"

"We can discover if we both fit on your stupidly small bed?"

15

EVERYTHING BETWEEN THEM had changed, it seemed, one second to the next.

Lisa wished the ride to her place had been longer. Now, when they were standing in front of her building, she should put a stop to this. She could tell him he'd be too distracting, which was the truth. If she took him upstairs, it would mean she really was going to confess everything. Not just her name, but the parts that mattered, as humiliating as they were. After all she'd learned about him—who he was at heart—she had to come clean if there was any chance for them.

Terrific time for her to decide she wanted a future with him.

It was hard to admit that a happy ending wasn't likely. She'd lied to him from the moment they'd said hello.

Still, there was a chance.

Once inside the building, her thoughts raced a mile a minute. How to start the conversation, how to keep her ex-client out of her confession.

"This is nice," he said, holding the elevator door for her.

It was just an elevator, nothing special, but there were no tags or graffiti. Even though there was no doorman, the

Intrigue Me

residents were mostly older or parents and did their best to keep the place clean. "I usually take the stairs." She pressed the button for her floor. "I steal exercise whenever I can."

"Very wise." He ran a hand down her back. "Which comes as no surprise."

No one was in her hallway, and she had her key out before they got to the door. Her hand didn't shake even when she remembered there was an envelope on the table that was addressed to Lisa McCabe. She'd have to move it ASAP. It had been stupid to bring him to her place. She wasn't ready.

"It's bigger than I expected." Daniel scanned the room, slowing when he looked at the bed and again at the table she used as a desk. "No wonder they have you filing. You're very organized."

"I like to think so." She put her key and the cash from her pocket into a small dish she kept on the table, her cell phone on a notepad. "Besides, there's no room to be messy." The envelope was right there, in her in-box. "Have a seat anywhere," she said, keeping her voice light as she lured him to the bed. She didn't take a breath until he plopped down.

Daniel was the first person she'd invited into her efficiency. She'd had to move there after Tess had wiped out her savings. The only reason she'd gotten the place was because Logan had cosigned and come up with first and last months' rent.

"Come sit," he said, patting the bed. "Tell me about the pictures on your wall."

The wall. Good. That was something to do. "I took those." Like a docent in her own museum, she sort of waved at the framed black-and-white prints and then went to the first photo. "These are my parents at the club where they live. They love golf above all things."

"Except you."

She thought about telling him why that wasn't necessarily true, but that seemed like too much information. Maybe after she'd bared all and the dust settled in their favor. "These beautiful pups are Jessie and Miley. They were our growing-up companions. Best friends ever. I miss having dogs."

"They're great at not spilling the beans." He nodded at the next photo. "And I suppose that good-looking guy is your brother."

"That's him. He's very smart. Most women get sidetracked by his looks, which he milks for all they're worth."

"I imagine a lot of people underestimate how clever you are, too."

"I can hold my own at *Jeopardy!*" Why hadn't she framed more pictures? There was nothing left to do but come clean. Well, there was one thing.

He grinned broadly as she finally sat down next to him.

"You're very good-looking," she said. "But I don't think you use that as your unfair advantage."

"No?"

"You don't have to. You're gifted. Celebrated. That's your ticket."

His hand froze inches from her hair. "Really? Do I play that up?"

"You don't need to. Everyone does it for you." She leaned closer to him and touched his cheek with the backs of her fingers.

When he kissed her, the distraction she'd hoped for didn't last. Instead, the repercussions of her lies, both outright and by omission, came to bite her in the ass. Her eyes burned with tears she refused to shed.

As their tongues stroked and teased, she couldn't stop herself from wondering how he was going to look at her

after she told him. Would he still want to touch her as if
she were someone special? Or worse, would he shrug it
all off because who she really was didn't matter? Never
mattered? He was as good as back at the Center and everything would change anyway.

Gripping his shoulders as if she could hold him forever,
she deepened the kiss until it was desperate. He moaned
into her mouth, held her close. She hated that her heart was
beating so hard because of fear when it should have been
love. But none of this was real. He needed to go back to
his life. Now that she'd seen him where he belonged, she
realized Eve was right to push. Daniel needed to take his
rightful place. Maybe Lisa had just been his vacation fling.

She had no room to complain or even be sad. This, them,
none of it was ever supposed to amount to anything.

"Honey," he whispered as they both caught their breath.
She had to close her eyes when he looked at her. "You
okay?"

She nodded. Smiled. "I…I'm glad you're here, but maybe
we should cool this down a little."

"Why?"

The confession stuck in her throat. Even after she cleared
it. Finally, she said, "You've had how much sleep in the last
forty-eight hours?"

Daniel's hand slipped under her T-shirt and he softly
ran his hand across her waist. His touch sent her worries
to a backseat when he cupped her bare breast.

"Oh, God," he whispered, kissing her shoulder then her
neck as he gently kneaded her, making her want him so
deeply it hurt. "You're gorgeous. Like silk. And Jesus, your
nipple is so hard for me." He moved his mouth to her ear,
where she could feel his warm breath. "I know where else
you're hard."

She'd thought bringing him up here would be a good

idea. And if they had sex maybe it would make it easier to confess. But she couldn't hide behind their postcoital glow.

"Daniel, wait." She leaned away, dislodging his hand from under her shirt. "You should get some rest before we go any further."

He smiled at her. "Thank you," he whispered, his expression raw and vulnerable. "For being there for me."

She swallowed. He was looking for comfort. She could give him that, even if this was the last time he'd want anything to do with her. Because afterward she had to tell him. Everything. The thought sent a shiver down her spine. Then her hand was behind his neck and she was pulling him into a kiss. He made this goofy little happy sound, which made her want to cry and never let him go.

When the angle finally got to them, and they had to move, he really looked at the bed. "Is this a…kid's bed?"

It was cheap and she'd never expected to sleep with anyone, and it fit her, so, why shouldn't she have a kid's bed. "It might be."

The smile he gave her was indulgent and confused, so everything was normal. For now.

"Take off your clothes," she said.

"What?"

"I know the bed is a challenge, but I think you're clever enough to make it work."

He stared at her, and she should've been ashamed, using him like this. His eyes were red and his face pale. But he also needed her. To be truthful, she needed him right back. God, this might be the last time for them.

"Challenge accepted." Before he took off a stitch, he grabbed hold of her bedding and yanked it back so hard most of it ended up on the floor. Then he pulled her close and kissed her.

She just hoped this second, or seventh, wind would last.

With her lips skating along his neck, she started pulling up his T-shirt. All she could think of was if she could somehow confess everything and make it sound glamorous. Or epic, or anything else that wasn't as horrible as the truth. This wasn't like TV, where people were forgiven for their sins before the hour struck. He was already dealing with his father's betrayal. He didn't need another one.

His shirt went flying. Except for her making him lift his arms, she doubted he even noticed. He seemed fascinated by her shirt. He kept shifting it from one shoulder to the other, then peeking down the front to see her boobs.

"You've seen them before. They haven't changed at all since the last time."

"Sure they have." He shook his head. "They're in your apartment, for one thing."

If she hadn't known better, she might have thought he was drunk. God, he was going to sleep forever. "Before we continue, is there a certain time you need to wake up?"

"Already put the alarm on my cell."

She smiled. This wonderful, remarkable ease they had. How was she supposed to let that go? "Tell you what," she said. "If you undress yourself, I'll take off everything but my T-shirt."

"Deal." He grinned as he undid his jeans.

This wasn't the plan. She was insane. She needed to tell him. Now. Not make love first. She owed him the truth.

By the time he'd stripped down to his boxer briefs, she hadn't moved.

"Um, have you forgotten our bargain?" He caught her hand and pulled her into his arms.

"I changed my mind. You should sleep first."

He brushed a kiss across her lips. "How about sex first, then sleep, then more sex?" Before she could answer he kissed her again, more deeply.

It was truly amazing. All the time they'd spent kissing, each one still felt like the first. Full of discovery and ever more passionate. As much as she hated to, she broke it off. "Have you eaten today?"

"You think I care about food right now?" he murmured against her lips. But things became more languid. Soft strokes of hand and tongue. She could tell he was drowsy.

"Here's my proposal," she said in a soft hypnotic voice. "I'm going to go fix us a light lunch and get us something to drink. I'm thirsty and you must be, too. Then you can go to sleep. If you can find a way to fit on the bed. Oh, and so we're clear. You're not going to sleep just because you're exhausted, but because I have work to do."

He groaned, clearly not liking that proposal one bit. "Work comes first. I get it. But you don't have to feed me."

She stepped back and turned toward the kitchen. "I hope you like tuna salad sandwiches, because that's all I've got."

"Sounds great," he said, the lie so obvious it would have been funny any other time.

Her kitchen wasn't much. Just a dorm-sized fridge, a countertop, a microwave and a toaster oven. Plus a coffeemaker, of course. A pony wall separated the area from the living room/bedroom.

Remembering the envelope with her name on it, she fought the urge to hide it and got the tuna and the bread out of the fridge. "I've got diet soda or beer."

"Beer, please."

That solved, she started making the sandwiches as she prepared herself for what was to come. She'd been a cop, and a good one, and she'd faced things a lot harder than making things right with someone she cared about. Even if he couldn't make peace with the truth, it wouldn't be the end of the world. It would just feel like it.

Her cell buzzed from her desk, and after she finished

the first sandwich, she took a look at who'd texted. She almost dropped the damn phone when she saw Heather's name.

Fleming a bust. Let's take another pass at Cassidy. TTYS.

It felt as though she was having a heart attack. Everything in her froze or burned, even the tips of her ears. Heather was supposed to be finished. Done. And Lisa didn't want her back. God, she knew so much more about Daniel now. Things she could have never learned from the best search engines or private investigators. The term was *intimate knowledge*. And she had that in spades.

Jesus, Daniel. She couldn't tell him a thing. Not today. Not until she figured out what this meant. At the very least, she needed to talk to Logan. She put her cell phone down and took the envelope from her in-box and socked it away in her desk drawer.

When she finally gathered the courage to look at Daniel, he was sound asleep. She'd never been more grateful.

16

DANIEL WAS STILL shaking off his strange morning when he arrived at the family home. It was a showpiece, of course, four stories with a view of Central Park. He had his key out before he remembered the place now belonged to Warren. Daniel would turn the key over to him before he left.

Instead of knocking, he took a minute. He'd spent most of the night at Lisa's sound asleep. The last thing he remembered, not counting this morning, was asking for a beer. Then it was somehow 2:00 a.m. and she'd kicked him out.

He smiled, remembering how sorry she'd been to wake him when his feet hung off the bottom of her ridiculously small bed, and his shoulders took up the top. They could have dealt with that if she hadn't had to go to work early. So, he'd made his way home, regretting the lost opportunity. Not just the sex, either. Time alone with Lisa had become a priority.

Once he'd gotten into his own bed, he should have fallen asleep right away, but thoughts about the visit to the cemetery kept him up. Not the part where he'd most definitely wanted Lisa to be with him. That, he'd deal with later. What had him staring at his dark ceiling was the way he'd felt after he'd blurted out all his fears. Warren would never have done such a thing. Neither would his dad. It seemed Daniel was taking all kinds of radical departures from the Cassidy rule book.

He'd tried to remember if Warren had ever loved the field. Maybe he did. Maybe, like Daniel, he would have chosen neurology on his own. But something told Daniel he wouldn't have. Yet he'd been a good son, even though Daniel had been the favored child. For God's sake, their dad had left Warren in the dark about the *big plan*. Daniel would see to it that it stayed that way.

At 6:00 in the morning he'd texted Warren that he'd like to meet him at the house ASAP.

Surprisingly, his brother texted back at 6:30 asking him to come by in an hour.

It was 7:24, and Daniel still couldn't decide what, if anything, he wanted to say to Warren. Could he ask him if he'd ever wanted to be anything else? Did he blame their mother for leaving? Would Warren tell him the truth? It wasn't any of Daniel's business. Just like it wasn't Warren's to tell him how to live.

There were three things Daniel knew for sure. One was that he didn't want to simply walk away from the clinic. The second was he didn't want to forfeit a full life for the work. And the third was he didn't want to lose Lisa. Although, he had a feeling the order was backward.

He knocked, and there was Warren, standing back to let him in, looking impeccable in his summer suit. "I see you have coffee. There's a fresh pot in the kitchen if you want more." He offered Daniel a packet of red sticky dots as they walked to the kitchen. "Mark what you'd like. I'll have the items sent to your house."

"What about what you want?"

"I've got green dots."

Daniel supposed that was fair since he'd dragged his feet. So he just nodded and stepped into the expansive, overdecorated kitchen. When they were little, it hadn't been this ostentatious. He remembered a lot of family breakfasts, a few lunches, hardly any dinners. But before school, he and Warren had eaten together. Their mother had never much cared for cooking, so they'd hired a lady to do it for her. The woman had been friendly and kept a secret stash of chocolate chip cookies just for him.

When Mom left, so did the cook. He'd been seventeen, Warren twenty-one.

Warren had poured his own refill. "Remember Angela's Dutch pancakes?"

Daniel did. So clearly he could practically smell the apples and the warm maple syrup. "I've never bothered ordering them at a restaurant. They would never come close."

"I'm assuming you don't want kitchen items?"

"No, thanks. I'd like to check out the office and the library. Maybe visit the atrium, not to take anything, just to visit. And my old room." As they started walking, Daniel asked, "You going to keep it?"

"I have a house. Besides, I've already signed with a Realtor. We're setting the price at 122 million."

"No way."

Warren shrugged. "She thinks it'll sell for at least that. Anyway, come on. I don't want to linger. And don't just mark the things you definitely want. If there's a question, put a dot on it. Furniture included. God knows you could use some of it in that mausoleum you live in."

"I've always liked the chairs in the library."

"Tag 'em. And don't forget the books are going to be sold. My bookshelves are as full as I want them to be."

Passing through the living room, Daniel had to laugh at what remained the most obvious piece of showmanship he'd ever seen. The centerpiece of the large glass table in the middle of a perfect room that looked out the glass doors to the garden and the water wall was an *Architectural Digest* with the cover shot of this room, looking straight out the glass door to the garden and the water wall. That magazine had held a place of honor since before the issue hit the stands.

There was also a gorgeous grand piano, which Warren would have marked as his. He'd played, while Daniel had studied the violin. Hated every minute of it, mostly because it distracted him from medicine, but now?

"If you're looking for the violin, it's in your old bedroom."

"How'd you know?"

"I grew up with you." Warren didn't stop until they reached their father's office. "And listen, if you want to take your time, I'll jot down the new security password for you."

"I don't want to keep you, but I'm glad that you're here." They were in the library, Daniel's favorite room. The bookcases climbed the walls. There was a wood-burning fireplace and the most comfortable chairs ever. He put a red dot on each one, and he didn't forget the ottomans. He thought about taking the coffee table, but didn't sticker it. "Does it still feel like home to you, Warren? Did it ever?"

"Yes. It did. There were lots of places to go when I didn't want to be bothered by my little brother. And we both knew how to manipulate the nannies. It was a good place to grow up."

"I'm not sure how I feel about it." Daniel brushed his hand over the long leather sofa before he put a dot on that, as well. "God knows we had everything we could ever want. But this place felt empty to me after Mom left."

Warren stopped to look at him. "You were younger, so I can understand that."

The antique carnival rocking horse hadn't been claimed until he put his red dot on it. "You talk to her much?"

Warren shrugged. "I told her we were selling the place, but she didn't want anything. When she divorced Dad, that was it for her. I thought she might want a share of the proceeds, but she didn't."

"It was nice of you to offer."

He went back to tagging. "You'll get your share."

"My share? The house belongs to you."

"122 million, Daniel. I think I can share some of it and still feed my children."

Daniel had never considered Warren greedy but his generosity still took him aback. Made him feel good. He didn't care about the money, though he wouldn't be stupid about it. He'd talk to his financial planner, make sure to donate a nice sum to the clinic, a couple of other charities he liked. Start trust funds for his kids. Future kids.

Lisa came easily to mind. Of course they'd never talked about wanting kids or not. He hadn't passed the wanting-sex-with-her-every-free-moment stage. But the way she spoke to patients and handled the children, yeah, he could see her as a mother.

Warren was eyeing him funny, so Daniel lost the goofy grin and got busy labeling hardback books, mostly first editions. Warren had chosen only one. *The Red Pony*.

Daniel raised his eyebrows.

Warren smiled. "I should have just taken it. It was the first book Dad ever read to me."

Daniel couldn't remember if his father had ever read to him. It didn't matter. He also tagged the chess set. It was hand-carved and beautiful, and he loved the game.

By the time he got to his room, the only thing of interest was his old violin. It was pricey and had a wonderful tone, but it had been years since he'd touched it. "Thanks," he said, warmed that Warren had kept it safe, locked in a glass case.

Warren nodded. "I've got to go." He handed Daniel a note with the password on it. "See yourself out, and remember, there's still coffee."

Daniel almost stopped him. But his brother left before he could gather the courage. Would Warren have been honest about his feelings toward Dad? Daniel had no idea.

He looked around his old room with the royal blue comforter on his queen-size sleigh bed and decided he didn't want it, even for a guest room. It didn't take him long after that to finish up, and as he grabbed one last cup of coffee, it hit him that Warren hadn't brought up the Center at all. Probably figured that now that he'd gotten a taste of working there, he'd never want to leave.

There was no denying how much he loved being there. God, to work with state-of-the-art equipment, to partner with brilliant specialists, to save lives that few hospitals in the world could tackle… All his years of study had been with one goal in mind. To be the best neurocritical specialist in the country.

But working at the clinic had opened his eyes to so much more. How much of life he truly wanted. He just hadn't figure out how to have them both.

Perhaps Lisa would help him find that balance. No, it was too soon to ask her something like that. If he had any right to at all. It would take all his courage just to ask her if she'd given any thought to their future.

When Daniel finally left, he thought about bringing her to see the place before it sold. That might seem too much like bringing her home to meet the folks. Although, he had already introduced her to Dad.

IT HAD BEEN fifteen hours since Heather's text. Lisa was actively working on another divorce case in the middle of a street fair in Park Slope, and she couldn't stop thinking about the mess she'd made of her life.

After Tess, she'd sworn she'd never get involved with anyone again. Not as a friend. Not as a lover. If she'd only stuck to her word, none of this would have happened. Heather would have found a reliable investigator, she'd have met Daniel and they would have clicked or not. Lisa would never have met him and never remembered how to care.

"It's also good for stretch marks and dark spots." The woman selling face oil was staring, first at Lisa then at the bottle she still held.

She put it down and said, "I'm going to do a little more shopping. I'll think about it."

The woman's shoulders slumped, but Lisa moved on, first locating Kevin Spitzer, the proud owner of four food trucks that worked all over Brooklyn and the cheating husband du jour. Lisa would be able to put this case behind her once she got the money shot of Kevin kissing his mistress, which should happen when he reached the end of market, where he and his mistress would likely meet.

Just the fact that he was there told most of his story. He was supposed to be in Manhattan, meeting with a chef. Instead, he was standing at the CRAZZZY HOT HOT SAUCE booth, eating sample after sample. She took another picture and silently willed him to move on already.

She'd situated herself between booths while she waited, her mind switching instantly to how she'd answered Heather's text with yet another lie. Middle of something. Talk soon. She could rationalize the reply, but she knew it was pure stalling while she tried to wiggle out of her situation.

Spitzer finally left the hot sauces behind him and

crossed to her side of the street. She trailed him slowly, wondering if perhaps the reason he was dawdling was because they weren't meeting until noon. It was 11:15 a.m. now. Damn it.

He'd stopped at a food truck, this one advertising their deep-fried candy bars. Kevin didn't look as if he was in tip-top shape. Especially in the beer-belly area. Not her problem. Thank God, because she had enough of her own.

Being trapped between the lies she'd told Daniel and the truth she may have to willfully omit in her conversation with Heather made her chest tighten and tied her stomach in knots. Add to that the hours she'd stared at Daniel asleep on her small bed while she cursed herself for ever entering the Moss Street free clinic, and she wished she could run away from home.

Kevin had eaten whatever ungodly mess he'd ordered, and now he was buying a magazine from a vendor. He didn't linger, which meant she didn't, either. When he reached the big corner flower shop, he stopped once more.

Bingo. The market ended with the flower shop, and it looked as if he'd ordered a bouquet of pink roses. Lisa took several pictures, staying just behind him, busying herself with a loaf of sourdough bread that smelled heavenly.

Just as Kevin took the bouquet, her phone rang. Lisa held her breath, hoping like hell it wasn't Heather. But she'd have been better off with her ex-client. The call was from Daniel, and she winced at each ring. She then counted the seconds until she found out if he'd left a voice mail or a text.

When the message was complete, she dutifully ignored it in order to make her camera ready. Kevin wasn't just standing at the corner—he was leaning against the wall, his flowers in one hand while he held the magazine with the other.

Lisa lined up the most likely shot. It wouldn't take long to just see the text message. She didn't have to answer it or anything. But she was more distracted by not looking than she would be if she just read it already.

Four clicks on her Android and there it was, nestled among two texts from Heather and three from Logan. She opened it.

Miss you. Hope everything's okay. Went to the house & met w/ Warren. Expected the worst but got surprised. Can't wait to tell all. Dinner?

Lisa looked over at the corner just in time to see Kevin and a woman kissing. By the time she took the picture, she captured the back of Kevin's shirt.

Cursing up a storm, she ran, trying to find them on the crowded street. Some idiot grabbed her by the shoulder, and she would have kicked the bastard in the nuts if it weren't for the sourdough loaf in her hand.

The man she'd almost kneed was actually a kid. And his mother was yelling "thief" from the booth.

"I'm sorry," she said, even though the boy didn't seem to care. He just walked beside her warily until she pulled out her wallet. "I'm so sorry," she said. "I didn't realize."

"You think you're the first to try that?" Although Lisa was directly on the other side of the long table filled with breads, the woman yelled at her as if she'd been in Queens. "This is New York. I don't give a damn what you did or did not realize. You stole my bread and almost got away with it."

"I'll pay for it now. Plus I'll add a baguette."

The woman, somewhere in her forties, huffed a laugh. "You'll add another two loaves if you don't want me making a fuss."

Lisa didn't argue. She paid the bill, held back the urge to apologize again and headed toward the only hotel in walking distance. Hopefully, this was just a nooner and they'd both come out the front doors in an hour. But with her luck lately, she'd probably watch all day for nothing.

"Great," she whispered, not paying a bit of attention to the bustling crowd on the street. "Now I'm screwing up *this* job." She tore off a big chunk of bread, took a bite and tried to find the best place to wait.

SHE SHOULDN'T HAVE COME.

She'd spent most of yesterday scrambling to find another way to get the picture she'd missed. A tip from Kevin's wife led her back to the hotel by the mostly empty farmers' market where she caught them pre-kiss, mid-kiss and post-kiss. A whole day wasted because she hadn't been paying attention, followed by another restless night. The few snatches of sleep she'd gotten had been plagued by nightmares, so she watched infomercials until it was time to shower.

Why the hell had she bothered coming all the way to the Bronx to do data entry? No, she hadn't wanted to flake out on Valeria, but Lisa wasn't exactly the cog that kept the wheel turning. At least she hadn't let anyone see her yet. She was still a block away, but with her luck, someone would catch her.

Lisa pulled her phone from her purse, but she didn't use it. She needed to think this through. She moved closer to the brick wall between shops.

She'd completed the paperwork on the divorce case this morning. She hadn't mentioned her blunder. No need for Logan to be disappointed in her when she was doing such a great job of it herself. The rest of her reports were up to date, and she'd already started the preliminary searches to track down another deadbeat dad.

So, maybe she should go enter data. Daniel had been at the Center since the night he'd slept over and Valeria had told her that they weren't expecting him today. Heather was still out of town. After several "Sorry, work" excuses, Lisa had told her they should meet to sign a new contract. In a text, of course. It had been radio silence ever since.

When she did return, Heather would probably want the new contract right away. Lisa had no grounds on which to say no to her, except that she'd been sleeping with the subject of her inquiry from the day after Heather had told her to switch her focus.

Of all of her mistakes, the only one that truly mattered was that she'd lied to Daniel, and now she'd been avoiding him. She'd barely slept the past two nights, and God, she needed to talk to Logan. He was the only one who knew everything that had happened to her, and without him, she'd have been lost.

She'd go by the office later, see if he'd returned yet.

Right, so go to the clinic? No? If by some fluke Daniel was there, she'd probably burst into tears and go hide in the bathroom until she could slink back to her apartment. Just like before. Just like after Tess.

Lisa shuddered as she remembered four long months of hopelessness. Of locking out the rest of the world. She'd worked, but only for Logan and only on cases where she didn't have to interact with anyone. It had taken all her courage to feel comfortable in a crowd, to engage in conversations. To volunteer. Then Daniel had broken through every barrier and she couldn't stand the thought of losing him.

So tense her jaw ached, she called the clinic. When Eve answered, Lisa nearly hung up and ran. Caller ID stopped her.

"Lisa. Hello."

"You're manning the reception desk?"

"Temporarily," Eve said, her voice so friendly, it made Lisa feel horrible. "I'm only here on my lunch break juggling the schedules."

Lisa winced. "About that... Would it screw up everything if I didn't come in today? I'm in the middle of something I can't get out of."

"Don't—"

"And also," she said, cutting Eve off. "Sorry, just... I won't be able to make it next week, either. At all."

"I understand. Your paying job comes first. I'll take care of it."

"Thank you," she said, relaxing. No reason to risk everything, just for filing.

"No problem," Eve said. "We'll see you when you're not so busy."

Lisa put the phone in her purse, ran a hand through her hair and took in the deepest breath she could. She'd go back to her place, check again to make sure—

She turned and her heart stopped.

Daniel was right there. Standing perfectly still, watching. Listening? He looked surprised and concerned. What had he heard? Another lie?

No, it wasn't technically a lie. She *was* in the middle of something. For all he knew, she could have been on a case. Logan could have called her back to Manhattan. She could leave right this second. Tell Daniel she had to go. He'd believe her.

She should. She really should. She couldn't.

The bridge to Daniel wasn't burned, not yet. Not completely. But one more manipulation might strike the final match.

"Do you have time for a cup of coffee?" he asked.

She swallowed, knowing that if she stayed, she might ruin everything anyway. But she couldn't say no. Not again. She met his gaze with a smile. "Sure. Coffee sounds good."

_17_

AT THE SMALL diner two short blocks from the clinic, Daniel gladly waited in line for their coffees while Lisa saved a table in the back. It gave him some time to think. He hadn't expected to see her from his taxi, and he definitely hadn't expected her stunned and frightened expression when she caught sight of him. Obviously, something was wrong. She seemed tense. Even jumped when he'd touched her arm. He might have let it go, assumed it was her job running her ragged, but she kept avoiding his eyes, and that was personal.

Even the smile she gave him as he sat across from her seemed forced.

She looked at her coffee, then at the blue walls. There weren't many other people in the seats, as most folks took their coffee to go. He hoped their relative isolation made her feel more at ease. Their last texts had been upbeat. But every time he'd tried to see her she'd had an excuse. Work. Perfectly understandable. Until now.

"You must've been on your way to the clinic," he said.

"No." She cleared her throat. "Actually, I just begged off today. Something's come up."

"Yeah, seems you've been busy," he said casually.

"Yep. You know, work. Hey, you were going to tell me about how it went with Warren."

He'd assumed she felt comfortable enough to say anything to him. That she clearly didn't twisted up his gut. "It went better than expected." He'd wanted to discuss his surprise at Warren's attitude and his ever-more-present need to make critical decisions about his life. But now? "It's weird that Warren's selling the place. He wants to give me half the proceeds, but I don't know. I'm still mulling that over. Dad left it to him."

"You never said much about the house. Is that where you grew up?"

"Yeah. It's on the Upper East Side. Park view. My father would have nothing less. I mean, Warren thinks it'll go for at least 122 million. It's a ridiculous price, but it was on the cover of *Architectural Digest.*"

Her blue eyes widened. "122 million? Dollars? It must be a palace."

"Almost. Certainly a shrine to my father's brilliance." His residual bitterness had lessened ever since the cemetery. "I can't blame him for it. He earned every penny he made by saving a lot of lives."

"No, I suppose not."

Daniel's cell phone buzzed. Eve's ring. He let it go to voice mail, but left the phone on the table. "Warren didn't bring up the Center once. I was surprised. We weren't ever close growing up, but for a while there in the house it felt like we were brothers. He not only put aside my old violin, I think he had it cleaned."

"That was nice of him." She glanced at him, then back to her utterly fascinating cup of coffee. "You play the violin?"

"Did play. Haven't since I went to Boston."

"You planning on taking it up again?"

He shrugged, very aware that she was keeping the spotlight on him. God, he wished she would just tell him what was on her mind. It was like talking to a stranger instead of his Lisa. She'd never been open about her personal life, but this was altogether different.

"That's great," she said, before he had a chance to turn the topic. "And Javier's surgery?"

The tightness in his chest cranked up a notch. "It went beautifully. We should be getting the results of the biopsy soon. In the meantime, his symptoms are gone. No more headaches, no more balance issues. He'll be able to go home tomorrow."

"So soon? That's amazing."

He leaned across the table and put his hand on hers. "Lisa? I… Something's wrong. I'm worried and I'd like to help if I can."

She looked away, but she didn't pull her hand back. She was struggling, though. The way she worried her bottom lip, the flush on her cheeks. Jesus, she wasn't going to break up with him. That would…that would hurt a lot more than he wanted to think about.

She looked up again and straightened her back in the chair. "The first day at the clinic, I was only there because I was working on a case. I never imagined myself volunteering, but I liked it. I liked the people, and to be honest, I liked you. The fact that I kept volunteering was a really big deal to me. I hadn't done anything like that since I quit being a cop."

Something cold tightened his chest. "I didn't know that. But I'm very glad you kept coming back." He paused, needing to tread lightly. "I'd gotten the impression that you hadn't left your job of your own free will."

Lisa didn't answer. Only stared into his eyes long enough that he worried she might bolt. Some kids were being obnoxious at the front of the diner. He wished they'd shut the hell up.

"I had my identity stolen," she said, the words coming hard and slow. "I was wiped out. All my money was gone. My savings. My credit was ruined. So much debt for purchases I never made."

"Oh—"

His phone rang again. He ignored it. Yes, he was late, but this was too important. "Christ. I'm so sorry."

Her pained smile told him his pity didn't come close to helping. "It was a big deal that I'd become a detective. I'd spent my entire career working harder than you can imagine to prove I hadn't gotten there on my looks. And I was good, too. Graduated with honors. First from the academy in academics and I kicked everyone's ass in tactical."

She shook her head but she still met his gaze. "God, I was so smug. I aced the detective exam. Worked like a demon to not just keep up but to be the best. Be the first out of my class to make detective. As you can imagine, I didn't have many friends."

He nodded, unwilling to interrupt. A few days ago she'd listened to him unburden himself. He suspected that was all she wanted from him now.

"It was all gone. In one day. My life. Gone. I didn't have a job. I couldn't pay the rent. The only reason I have anything now is because of my brother."

They both took a breath. He squeezed her hand, and she took a sip of her coffee. "I can't imagine," he said. "But you mentioned you quit. You weren't fired. So why aren't you still—? If it was something political, Warren knows the chief of police, and—"

"Daniel," she said. "I appreciate it. I do. But I really did resign. Nothing political, nothing… I was a detective in the Grand Larceny Unit, specializing in identity theft.

I was supposed to be the best. And I let it happen to *me*. There's no coming back from that."

He inhaled as the ramifications of what she'd said finally hit him. "How long has it been? Because you seem pretty well-adjusted, considering…" He thought about that shoe box of an apartment. "You know you can always stay with me. No strings—"

His phone rang for a third time. Okay. He'd call Eve soon.

"Do you need to get that?"

"No."

"Okay." She slowly nodded. "Look, again, thanks for the offer. It's so kind. But here's the thing. When my life was ripped away, I knew I could never trust anyone or anything again. When I say my identity was taken, I mean that in every sense of the word. Before I met you, I hadn't been on a date in well over a year. I hadn't even put myself in a situation where I could get close enough to a guy.

"I never expected you. That we had sex at the clinic… Oh, my God, I can hardly believe that. But it's even more difficult to fathom you. Us. I wasn't prepared. And I got scared."

The band in his chest barely let him catch his breath. She was leaving him. Right now, in a coffee shop.

"I'd been mourning the loss of, well…me," she said, her words carefully convincing him he was right. "I still am. I like you so much and I don't want to leave, but—"

"No. I understand. I truly do. More than most. I'll back off. I will. I won't press at all. However long it takes. I'll wait until you're ready."

Lisa had rarely seemed vulnerable to him, but she did now. And then his damn phone rang again. It was Eve, only this time it was a text. All it said was 911.

"Shit. There's an emergency at the clinic. I have to go." He stood up, and so did Lisa. He pulled her into his arms and kissed her. He held her closer when she kissed him back. Maybe all wasn't lost. Even though it had felt like it a second ago.

She was the first to pull away. "You should go."

"Will I see you later?" he asked.

She winced. "I really do have to work. I'm not sure."

He hated leaving her like that. He ran the two blocks, wondering if he was making a huge mistake.

LOGAN WAS LATE. He'd texted he'd be in the office around 5:00 and she'd been in the hallway, pacing, since 4:30. The only break was when Daniel had texted that he'd be home between 7:30 and 8:00. Which meant he'd like her to come over. She missed the way those texts had lifted her spirits and made her tingle with anticipation. This mess had to be over soon or she'd go nuts. At least they were still texting like a couple of schoolkids. Regrettably, this response would be very much like the last. Not sure yet. When the elevator dinged at 5:13 p.m., the tension that had given her a headache and an upset stomach eased a little.

"How long are you going to be here?" she asked.

Logan looked worn-out and dusty in his khaki pants and tan shirt, his equipment heavy on his shoulder and in his hand. As he got closer she could see he had shadows under his eyes.

"Not long. What's going on?"

She had no business holding him up. "Nothing. It'll wait until—"

He turned from the door, key in hand, to look at her. Lisa tried to appear as if her world wasn't crumbling around her, but she must have failed, because he opened the door and said, "Come on in."

"Seriously, I can—"

"Come in. Sit down. And tell me what's going on. You look like hell."

"Yeah."

He got a couple of sodas from the fridge, gave her one and then sat behind his desk. She took her regular seat and began the speech she'd been practicing since she'd left the coffee shop this afternoon. "We had this…unusual client. The one who had me look up—"

"Trading Cards, right?"

"Yes," she said. "This client, Heather—"

"The cheapskate?"

"Are you going to keep interrupting?" she asked, even though his butting in made her feel oddly better.

"Am I right?"

"Yes." She fake coughed "Egotistical smart-ass," but didn't execute it very well, her cough stopping halfway into the first word. But she knew it didn't matter. He was her big brother, and he'd help her.

"I might interrupt again. But go on. I'll try to hold back."

She leaned forward. "This is important to me, so yeah. I'd like you to really listen."

Logan nodded slowly. "You know I have your back, right?"

"Yes. You're the one person I can truly count on. So it's hard for me to tell you the whole story here."

"Just go for it. I won't love you any less."

If only she could hear that same thing from Daniel. "Okay, Heather, who paid for the basics, is back again after we closed out her account. She'd gotten exactly what she paid for the first go-round, on both men, and she went for the second one."

"But…?"

"But now she wants to pay for the complete package on the first doctor. Public records, background checks, everything. And I'd have to disclose that I knew about this doctor's relationship with a medical center."

"Oh, for God's sake, Lisa, you're not being cross-examined. I assume this is the doctor you like. What was his name…Daniel? And she didn't even know you'd gone to the free clinic, let alone… What's the medical center?"

If she had trouble telling Logan, how was she going to tell Daniel? Maybe she should just move to another state and start over again. "His father started the Madison Avenue Neurological Center. But he died three months ago, and now it belongs to Daniel and his brother, Warren. When Heather hired me, I knew that his father and brother had owned it. But Daniel wasn't working there, so I didn't tell her."

"You weren't required to."

"But he's brilliant and has all the credentials. Of course he was going to end up at the Center."

"Of course? No. You're speculating. Daniel might have had a falling-out with the brother. He could have changed his mind about his future. Anything that wasn't the fact that he worked at a free clinic wasn't your concern. In fact, you don't even have to work with her ever again."

"She'll probably just hire someone else."

"Who would tell her the facts about his employment at the time he or she investigated."

Lisa sighed. "I know you're right. But I can't be certain the real reason I didn't tell her wasn't because I was speculating."

"I know, kiddo. You really like this guy."

She nodded and wasn't sure why she felt embarrassed. Probably because what she felt was so much more than just liking him. "I don't want you to get sued or anything. So what do I tell her?"

"She can't sue. What you tell her is up to you. But if you decide you really like and trust this guy, then—"

"I know. I have to tell him the whole thing right away." She felt sick at the thought. But having not told him yet was her biggest worry. Forget about Heather. That Daniel had taken her to his father's grave, had trusted her to hear the thing he was most afraid of… Would he even want a friend who couldn't tell him the truth, let alone a lover?

"Thanks, Logan," she said, standing, taking her first drink of the soda she'd been holding.

"Sure there's nothing else you want to tell me?"

"I'll tell you how it ends—how's that?"

"Remember. You're the brave one. Always have been."

She'd saved him from drowning at Brighton Beach when they were kids. He'd never let her forget it. "Not always."

He stood up, too. "Tonight seems like a perfect night for courage."

For his first trip back to the clinic in several days, he hadn't been too slammed with patients, but his notes seemed to be taking forever. It still bothered him that he'd had to cut short the talk with Lisa, but it was a good thing he'd arrived when he had. A woman in the waiting room had slurred speech, a terrible headache and nausea. Although it presented as an ischemic stroke, a few tests revealed she was suffering from a very severe migraine.

Eve had been all set to give him hell for making her call three times, but then he told her he'd been with Lisa. Something must have hit her strangely about his expression or his tone because she hadn't said another word.

Having to leave Lisa that way had him feeling jumpy. He had tremendous sympathy for what she'd been through. But he had no way to fix it.

"Dr. Daniel?"

He looked up from his final patient's notes. "I won't be another minute, Hector."

"No, sir. It's not… There's a lady. She says she's not here for an appointment, but she wants to see you?"

"Okay…you sound as if something might be wrong. Does she appear to be ill?"

"No. She's really dressed up. Like for a party or something."

Daniel frowned. "I think I can handle it, but thanks for the warning. Just send her in."

Who did Daniel know that would come here all dressed up? Well, Lisa had, but that hadn't been on purpose. God, she'd looked hot.

There was a light tap at the door, and the woman entered. He didn't know her. Hector had been right about her being dressed up. Her brunette hair was in some kind of fancy twist; her makeup looked expertly applied. Although her dress was close-fitting, red and strapless, it wasn't immodest in any way. She reminded him of Warren's wife. Of a lot of doctors' wives.

"Dr. Cassidy," she said, holding out her hand. He took it, but he didn't miss a second of her head-to-toe examination of him. "Heather Norris."

"Have we met?"

She shook her head and then took a seat in the blue wing chair, crossing her ankles and resting her feet at an angle. "No, we haven't. I admit I'm breaking the rules somewhat by coming to meet you without an introduction."

"What rules?"

She didn't shrug, but she did move one shoulder forward, which did interesting things to her bodice. "The Hot Guys Trading Cards. All those women scrounging for cards, it wasn't for me. But I was stunned to find out that a man like you would make yourself available like that."

"I'm afraid you've mistaken me for someone else. I haven't a clue what you're talking about."

Ms. Norris looked honestly surprised. "I was told all the men on the cards had to give their consent."

This was getting weird. "What cards?"

She opened her purse and pulled out what looked like a baseball card. He was forced to go to her to get it, and he didn't make it back to his seat when he really looked at it. His picture was on the front. His name and the clinic's phone number were on the top right, another name and number on the top left. Josephine Suarez. It sounded familiar, but he couldn't place it.

The back of the card made him sit down. It was exactly what Ms. Norris had said. A trading card. But a damn weird one. It got his career right, but then it stated that he wanted to get married, that his favorite restaurant was a home-cooked meal, that his passion was using his skills to help people, and then came something called the bottom line, whatever the hell that meant. It said "Has a great heart."

"What the hell is this?"

"You really didn't know about the card? How is that possible?" Her confused expression seemed genuine. "Looks like I hired Lisa for nothing," she murmured.

"Lisa?" He studied the woman more closely. "Who are you?"

She blushed. "I'm sorry for the misunderstanding. I assure you, I would never have come here if I'd known the card was made without your consent." She put her hand on the arm of her chair, but she didn't stand. Instead, she looked at him once more, this time with an arched eyebrow and a hint of a smirk. "Do you have time for a drink?"

It was just past 6:30. He would have said no in a heartbeat if she hadn't mentioned Lisa. But she had, and he wanted to know why. "Sure."

18

LISA KEPT STARING at her cell phone. It was after 8:00 and she still hadn't heard from Daniel.

She'd texted him twice since he'd told her he'd be home by now, and the second one had said Your place, I assume?, which he should have confirmed. Even if something was going on at the clinic or the Center, it wasn't like him to leave things so unclear. In fact, she could think of only one time he'd been this late texting her about them getting together, and that was because he'd forgotten his cell phone in a different jacket.

Maybe she should call him? Make sure they were still on for the night? After her talk with Logan, she'd been encouraged. Not enough to take her overnight things, though. History had taught her not to rule out Daniel's decision not to accept her apology. If she'd been the one to suddenly discover he'd been using a false name and more, she'd be hard-pressed to forgive and forget. Unless there was a damn good reason.

The only reason she had for any of her foolish moves was fear. Would he understand? Could anyone who hadn't been through it truly know what it was like to be stripped to the bone of everything you'd believed to be sacrosanct?

To find yourself with no means to eat, no roof over your head, no job? All at the hands of your best friend in the world?

A number of people knew about what had happened to her. Everyone on the team of detectives working to find out who killed Tess and how she'd managed to do so much damage using one of the most sophisticated computer systems in the country. A few people had a good idea why Tess's actions had led Lisa to resign from the NYPD. But she'd told her entire story to only one person, and that was her brother. He knew every last humiliating, devastating detail.

Now she was going to tell Daniel. There were things she wanted to leave out but she wouldn't. The story would make her look like a fool, but that was the deal here. If they were to be more than just friends with benefits, she'd need to start with a clean slate. He deserved to know exactly who she was and who she'd been.

At least one troubling situation was behind her for the time being. She'd texted Heather, asking for a meeting tomorrow or the next day. Lisa doubted she'd still want her services. It wouldn't hurt her feelings if Heather got angry. The woman was a cheater and money hungry to boot.

Lisa checked her watch again. If he wasn't there by 8:30, she'd call him one more time.

Three minutes later, a taxi pulled up in front of his home. With fear in her blood, she stood up, panic warring with her attempt to act naturally.

When she saw the look on Daniel's face as he approached, her heart nearly stopped.

"I WASN'T SURE you'd be here." Daniel unlocked his front door. He knew his voice sounded hard and distant, but there was no way he was going to pretend that he hadn't learned the truth about Lisa, if that was her real name. Or that it hadn't hurt him to the core.

"I didn't hear back from you." She sounded like the vulnerable lover he'd felt so sorry for at the coffee shop. Was it an act? Had everything been an act?

"I was meeting a mutual acquaintance."

"Sorry, what?"

He stepped into his house, still not sure what to do next. "Heather Norris. Name ring a bell? Our conversation was very enlightening."

"Heather... She called you?"

Daniel's chest hurt. How much had he wished Lisa wouldn't recognize the name. That she was innocent of Heather's charges. "No. She came to the clinic. Showed me a trading card with my name on it. My real name. Pity I don't know yours."

Lisa swayed to the right, and he readied himself to catch her if she started to fall, but he needn't have bothered. He couldn't be certain due to the quality of the outdoor light, but she looked very pale. He'd be pale, too, if he'd lied about who he was to someone who'd fallen...who'd cared about him.

"I really do need to talk to you," she said. "I had no idea Heather would contact you. I came here to explain—"

"Maybe another time," he said, not in the mood to hear more bullshit. "I'll call for a taxi."

"No, wait. Please. I know you're shocked and angry. I have no idea what Heather said to you. She barely knows me, and I don't know her. But I do know you, and I'd like to explain. To tell you what I wasn't able to this morning. Especially the parts where I was an idiot. And then I'll go. No matter what you feel right now, please, I need to tell you."

He closed his eyes. He wanted her to come in. To straighten everything out so he could understand what she'd done, but he wasn't sure that was possible. He'd tried to explain it all to himself, used the excuse that they'd run out of time when he'd had to go to the clinic, but for God's sake, he'd taken her to his father's grave and he didn't know her *name*.

He was probably subjecting himself to yet another round of torture, but he stepped back.

She walked in, making sure they didn't touch as she passed.

Heather had said she'd fallen for Lisa's spiel. The woman had been angry, and once he heard her story he understood why. The security firm Lisa's brother owned looked completely legit. But Lisa had only taken her case in order to snag him for herself. Drain him dry and then move on to the other doctor on Lisa's list.

He'd known colleagues who had experienced precisely that. Dangerously good actresses whose sole interest was money. So it wasn't all that hard to believe, except… He clamped down on that thought. He had no idea who Lisa truly was, only what he wanted her to be. "I saw your website," he said, as she made her way carefully to the living room.

"You took down the airplanes."

Daniel's hands fisted. "Don't talk about my home. In fact, just…sit down. I'll be back. I don't think I can hear this without a drink."

The kitchen offered him a little relief. At least he couldn't see her. Looking at her face, so familiar he'd been able to read every emotion in her gaze, was too much to handle. Ironically, he wanted to hire a private investigator to find out everything he could about Lisa McCabe. And Lisa Pine. And whatever other name she went by. Christ, he'd been a first-class idiot.

He poured himself a scotch. It took a while for him to clear his mind. Images of her in his bed. Naked and gorgeous, falling apart as he brought her to climax. Kissing her until they'd both been breathless. How she must have laughed at him when she went home.

He brought the glass to his lips, but didn't drink. They'd had sex in the clinic. He doubted he'd lose his license over it, but it would be a nasty scandal. Maybe she meant to blackmail him. Too soon to tell.

When he finally got it together, she stood where he'd left her. "Go ahead," he said. "Say what you need to say."

Her face was as beautiful as it was tragic. No matter who she turned out to be or how real that expression was, he was so close to helpless around her that he had to hang on to his drink before he fell.

"I told you a lot about what had happened to me when I was a detective. Every word of it was true. You won't find it on any website, though, because the files at One Police Plaza had been breached, and they clamped down on that the moment they became aware. It didn't happen only to me, but it did happen because of me."

Nowhere to look it up, then. As an opening gambit, that didn't sit well. Daniel sipped his scotch and tried his best not to meet her gaze. He didn't succeed.

Interestingly, she didn't cross her arms or try to cover herself in any way. Her arms were down at her sides where she rubbed her thumbs obsessively against the side of her palms.

"The person who hacked the personnel files of five employees including me was someone I knew. She wasn't working alone, but she sat at the helm of all the havoc. Her name was Tess Brouder, and she was my—" She took a deep breath. "She was my best friend.

"We met in the academy. Bonded right away. There weren't that many women in our group, but I think we would have been friends regardless. She was easy to talk to, funny, sarcastic. I helped her with the physical stuff—she wasn't very strong, but she was determined. She helped me with the more personal side of things. We got an apartment together. Worked our asses off, but there was one thing we didn't share.

"I was hit on all the time. I don't know why, except for the obvious, but it wasn't just the guys in our class. It was instructors and goddamn people who should have known better. I didn't realize it then, but I was still threatening. I understood it in high school and college, but I thought that part would change when I became a cop. It didn't. I was a threat to other women, to men—especially those who were struggling in areas where I excelled. Looking back, I was naive. I kept my nose to the grindstone and did my best.

"Tess was the only one I could talk to about it. But I didn't think. It never happened to her. She was pretty in her own way, but she didn't attract much attention. She was fierce in my defense and in chasing men away. She made sure we were together almost all the time. She made my life so much easier.

"I'd never had a friend like her before. I would have done anything for her. I trusted her like I'd never trusted anyone. She knew my deepest secrets."

Daniel finished his drink. Her story sounded extremely familiar. Not getting hit on, but he knew the kind of men she was talking about, so he couldn't find fault with that. But the trust thing? Lisa knew more about him than Warren. Than Eve. Maybe this was some kind of revenge. It wasn't out of the question.

Although, my God, she had to be an extraordinary actress because he could see the pain she was in. Feel it. Even after all he knew, he wanted to rescue her. Was it the power of her beauty? It certainly had been her looks at the start. He'd seen her and that was it—he wanted her. Maybe that had been the catalyst. That he was just one more dick who cared about her only because of her beauty. If that were true, he could almost understand it.

"Then I discovered my bank accounts had been drained completely, my credit cards stolen and used in a way that even though the banks forgave some of it, I was stuck with a mountain of debt. Our rent hadn't been paid in months. But I didn't connect Tess with any of it. It never occurred to me that she was the only person who had that kind of access to my life. She acted as if she was as devastated as I was by the theft.

"Unfortunately, the people who had to know what happened so they could investigate were the people I worked with. I was part of the team. No one could look me in the eyes. I tendered my resignation immediately. My brother helped me, but when I found out that it was Tess that did it…" She shook her head and looked away from him for the first time since she'd begun her speech. A moment later, she looked up again.

"She was murdered, by the way. Executed. The reason hasn't been determined. One thing the detectives discovered in the apartment where she was hiding was a flash drive containing a diary."

The last word had broken, and it looked as if Lisa was broken, as well. It would have been so easy to hold her. Soothe her. But he still couldn't understand what that trading-card thing was about. What he'd heard from Heather. Why Lisa had come to the clinic at all, when Heather had paid for only an internet search.

If all this was true then she'd had plenty of time to tell him that she'd given him a false name. Why wait so long? Had she planned never to tell him? Was she finally talking because Heather spilled everything?

He'd honestly thought he could love Lisa. He probably already did. Otherwise, it wouldn't hurt this much.

"I—"

"Just wait. I need time to think."

She paused, bit her lower lip. He wished she'd stop.

Finally, she broke the silence. "That's basically it. I came to the clinic because your education didn't make sense. I had no intention of volunteering until you asked what I was doing there. Then, I don't know, I got scared and used my mother's maiden name instead of McCabe."

Her attempt at a smile nearly did him in. "It was supposed to be a fling. My first attraction in years, and definitely the first since I'd holed up in my efficiency. You were there for the rest, except the part where I realized I was falling for you. That was scary, but then, almost everything was. When you changed the rules on me, I don't know. It all caught up with me. I thought the name was the least of it." She sighed and tears traced down her cheeks. "There's no reason for you to believe me. I don't even blame Heather for whatever she did."

"Can you at least explain about that? About Heather?"

Lisa shook her head. "I'm sorry. I can't talk about a client."

He chucked out a bitter laugh. "What, private-detective-client confidentiality? That's a new one."

She seemed to be held together by sheer will. She wiped her face clean as she walked to the couch, but she didn't look at him until after she'd taken her purse and pulled out her cell phone. "I hope you can believe that I'm sorry. You've been wonderful. I was actually—" Her shoulders fell. "I'll find my way home."

He stood, but he didn't move. She did, though. She walked out and closed the door behind her.

The urge to give chase was there in his chest, all the

way to the bone, but he honestly didn't know if he could trust himself around her.

He wanted to believe everything she'd said. He could almost hear his father laughing at him.

THE TEXT ON Lisa's monitor blurred. Again. Damn tears and the way she couldn't turn them off. It hadn't helped that she'd stayed up all night, going over and over what she'd done wrong.

The words from Tess's diary had spelled it all out. Her "friend" had listed her faults in stunning detail. Lisa had tried not to believe them at the time, but now they came back to mock her: Selfish. Thoughtlessly cruel. Egotistical. Narcissistic. The most repeated accusation was that every achievement of Lisa's hadn't been an achievement at all. Just others letting her win. Teachers giving her higher grades than she deserved. Men wanting her because of her looks and nothing more.

She wasn't convinced she was all of those things, but some of them made her squirm.

Although…Daniel wasn't some idiot to be manipulated. He was brilliant. Far more brilliant than anyone she'd ever met. He might have had sex with her because he was attracted to her, but why on earth would he take her to his father's grave if she was nothing but arm candy?

And why had he believed her yesterday at the coffee shop and not last night? What had Heather said? Despite how it looked, Lisa had meant no harm. By any other name, she was still Lisa. And her heart was just as vulnerable.

He'd surprised her yesterday. All she'd wanted to do was tell him the truth, but then he was gone, and she hadn't had a chance to tell him everything. Now, of course, she realized she shouldn't have said anything until she'd had time to think.

That was what he'd asked for. Time to think. And all she wanted was to stop thinking. Everything in her hurt. Her bones, her muscles, her skin. Her eyes burned; her lower lip was a wreck. She'd thought she'd lived through the worst pain of her life. Wrong, wrong, wrong. She'd tried so hard not to love him. But she'd failed at that, too.

Was it too early to start drinking? Screw it. People had Bloody Marys for breakfast. She could have some Jack. It would take the pain away. Had to, because she couldn't live with this.

The kitchen was five steps away, and she couldn't find the will to take them. She'd done her very best. Broken all her rules to be with him. The hell with Tess's diary, Lisa had been a friend when Daniel had needed one. Why wasn't he looking at the evidence? She'd never asked him for anything.

There had to be something she could feel aside from heartache and self-pity. She'd tried, hadn't she?

The volunteering part had been good, even without Daniel. There were free clinics all over New York, so maybe she'd do that again. Meet some people. Be more careful, that was all. Keep her distance.

Still, maybe she should try getting together with old friends first. There weren't many. But she'd already broken through the awkwardness with Cory, so he seemed like a logical choice. She took a deep, hitching breath and picked up her cell phone. Did she have his personal number? She looked at her contacts, and there it was.

The thought of texting him made her pulse beat even harder, but come on, she wasn't going to die because Daniel didn't want her. It only felt as though she was dying. Eventually, it would get better. That would happen faster if she made an effort. That was human nature, right?

Cory it was. She texted him something easy. Nothing too scary. Maybe we could catch lunch sometime?

Despite all her willpower, she only managed to save it. She'd send it the moment she was ready. Okay. She'd done an almost brave thing on the worst day of her life. That had to count for something.

She tried once more to read the case file on her monitor. Nope.

It was time to cry uncle. Her heart had been broken, so today would be about feeling sad. Maybe tomorrow, too. But not longer than a week.

Her chuckle sounded off. Like a record on the wrong speed. Because a week would never be enough.

19

IT HAD BEEN three days since that horrible night, and Daniel had managed to wind himself up into an ever-tightening ball of confusion, guilt and remorse. He'd been tempted to call Lisa so many times it was crazy, but he didn't want to make things worse, so he held off.

Just this morning he'd written her texts out of habit. Just as he'd done the day before. For reasons he barely understood, instead of deleting the small missives, he saved them. He wondered if she was doing the same thing, which was ludicrous. Why would she? He'd sent her away very effectively.

That was where guilt kicked in. Which was happening more and more, and now there were different kinds of unanswerable questions in the mix. If they did get back together, would she ever trust him again? Or had his dismissal pushed her back behind the walls she'd finally managed to escape? If any of that story was even true.

He walked over to the window that took up a large portion of two walls. The view was as spectacular as his father's crazy dreams. Daniel had an unimpeded view of the reservoir in Central Park.

Lisa had been right, whether through honesty or guile: he'd found nothing about a break in police security online. The name Tess Brouder had a few mentions, but those turned out to be from local papers from her high school years, if that was the same woman. There was no death certificate in the public records, and Daniel wasn't sure what to make of that.

He missed Lisa more deeply than he'd known was possible, which made him so angry he wanted to scream. Thoughts of her kept him up late and visited his dreams when he did find sleep. During the day, the texts were only part of it. Moss Street wasn't the same. No one thought or said anything about it because no one knew. Though some of the staff were calling him Dr. Cassidy again. Probably because he'd reined himself in behind his shield of position and status.

His change in demeanor wasn't notable at the Center, but that was only because Warren wore that stiff mantle all the time.

Daniel picked up the next file on his desk at the Center. He still didn't feel 100 percent comfortable. In the imaging room, he was in the zone, but here, in Warren's old office, he couldn't settle. His brother had taken over their father's office, and now that Dr. Elliot had pushed back his retirement for another year, he had the office that was to have been Daniel's. It felt off. Wrong. Even he recognized his discomfort was because of his father's absence.

A tap at his door was followed immediately by Eve walking in.

"Come in," he said as sarcastically as he could.

It didn't faze her. Why did he even try?

"Here," she said, handing him an elegantly wrapped gift.

"What's this?" Of course he knew what was in the box. A tie. She hadn't wrapped one in a long time, though.

"Open it."

"What's the occasion?" He pulled the ribbon, not paying it much attention. Eve had made herself comfortable in one of the guest chairs. There were no blue velvet wing chairs, but the price of one of the Louis XV chairs could keep the clinic running for a month.

"You're coming to work here permanently in two weeks. I thought it was time for a change."

Shaking his head at Eve's not so subtle way of telling him it was time to take his place at the Center emotionally as well as physically, he guessed she'd have gotten him something from Prada or D&G. When he opened the box, he sat back, startled. Then he laughed as he held up the tie. "Tweety Bird?"

"That's the first laugh I've heard out of you in a while. You want to tell me what happened to Lisa?"

"No. Nothing happened to her. She was an illusion. Whatever she told you and me was myth."

"That's a pretty serious accusation."

"Based on her own admission. She went to the clinic to investigate me. For a client. I was part of some underground trading-card group. I meant to ask you if the name Josephine Suarez means anything to you."

Eve closed her eyes as she sighed. "Oh, for heaven's sake. You know her as Josie. Valeria's sister. She's one of our semi-regular volunteers. There was some sort of requirement to submit an eligible bachelor, and she used you. Her intention was to get the card back immediately, but as time went on with no calls to her, she believed the card was lost."

"And you know this because…?"

"She confessed to Valeria when she lost track of the card. It was a foolish thing to do, but she meant no harm. I should have told you, but it seemed like a moot point by the time I heard about it."

"You can let her know that I ripped the damn thing to shreds."

"I will. So you believe that this trading card led Lisa to the clinic?"

"I know it did. She gave a false name. Don't we check driver's licenses or anything when someone volunteers?"

Eve studied him for a long moment. "That must have been awful."

"I said I tore up the card."

"I meant about Lisa. You two were really good together."

"I'm fine. Look, I don't want to talk about this, all right?"

Eve tapped a finger, her brows furrowed. Then she finally said, "Have you spoken to a designer about remodeling this office?"

"No."

"You really expect me to believe you'll be happy working out of Warren's old office without changing a thing?" She nodded at the gilded nightmare of a Louis the-something-or-other desk. "That monstrosity belongs in a museum. Literally."

"What," he said, "you don't like ormolu drawer pulls?"

"The point is you don't. Please talk to me, Daniel. You'd been so happy. Did she really lie about everything? That just seems impossible."

He didn't want to rehash his very real nightmare, but if there was one person in the world he could truly trust, it was Eve. So he started at the beginning of the end. The day at the cemetery. He didn't tell Eve what he'd said about his father, just what it felt like to trust Lisa so much.

When he reached the part about how he'd told Lisa to leave, he could barely look at Eve. He closed his eyes when he asked her all the questions he'd been asking himself, including the one that bothered him the most. "How could she not tell me her name? I would have understood, if she'd only told me what was going on from the start."

"Daniel," she said, shaking her head. "You're so very smart, but sometimes that big brain of yours doesn't do you any favors. I believe the expression is 'can't see the forest for the trees'?"

"I really can't deal with a life lesson right now, Eve. Just please, if you see things more clearly than I do, tell me. I honest to God don't know what to do."

"Okay. Tell me something. How did you feel when you were with her?"

His chin hit his chest. He debated changing the subject. Refusing to answer. But in the end he did as she asked. "Wonderful," he said. "Grounded. Happy." He looked at Eve again. At her steady gaze. "Lisa was different. She didn't care about money or the clinic or where I'd gone to school. I wanted that. Her. I was more like myself with Lisa than I've ever been. But don't you get it? That's why it hurts so much. Who the hell was I with? Lisa Pine or Lisa McCabe? Or someone else she would make up tomorrow?"

"There was something you said earlier." Eve's voice was calm, unlike his. "Try to imagine if everything you now have in your professional life was taken away. Stolen from you. If no one cared that you'd been at the top of your classes and won coveted awards. What if it didn't matter that you've saved so many lives? That you were *you*." Eve paused. "Now, imagine it was me who betrayed you."

Daniel experienced a physical reaction. As if he'd received a blow to his chest.

Eve smiled gently. "That's who came to the clinic that day. A woman stripped of her identity in every way that counted. Now that I know the depth of her betrayal by her closest friend, I would have been stunned if she'd told you her real name. What astonishes me more is that she let you into her heart. What a risk she took.

"Trust me when I say Lisa is in love with you. Her false name is a symptom, not the cause. And you can just toss out every single thing Heather said. Her only agenda was to snag herself a rich doctor. She had no idea who she was talking about. But you do."

Tears burned at the backs of his eyes, and that hadn't happened in years. Not even at his father's funeral. He went back to the window, although he saw nothing but Lisa. For a long time, he thought about what Eve said. About what life would be like without the woman he loved.

The sky was ablaze with color when he finally said, "The courage it must have taken for her to stand in front of me like that. When she knew I'd already made up my mind. Even then she bared the most damaged part of herself, holding nothing back. I should be so brave."

"You are that brave," Eve said. "You went and found your own path when everything was against you. I'm immensely proud of you, and that won't ever change. But if you truly understand Lisa, you know that she's in a lot of pain right now, and you're the cure."

"What if it's too late?"

"All you have to do is tell her the truth. All of it. And you'll be fine."

He moved from the window and did something he hadn't done in years. He hugged Eve. "Thank you."

"No sweat. Now go on and get her."

LISA WALKED SLOWLY on her street. It would be dark in a few minutes and she probably should have hurried, but she didn't care. Today had been about as boring as her job could get. She'd had to wait in a Starbucks, by the window, watching the bank across the street. The man she was looking for was supposedly going to cash out his life savings, leaving his family penniless, while he then took off for Bali.

It was hateful. She'd had too many cups of coffee, then soda, then coffee again. Too many pastries, and far too much time to think about Daniel. She did see the man. She did call Logan, who then carried on without her. Now she was full, and all she wanted was to veg out in her luxury apartment and watch her fifty-inch HDTV. Unfortunately, she had to go back to her real apartment.

Missing him was a permanent ache now. A piece of her heart cut out, only the phantom pain remaining.

As she approached her building, she saw a man standing near the door. His back was to her, but she knew without one iota of doubt that it was Daniel. Her crippled heart thudded in her chest and for a few glorious seconds she thought everything would turn out exactly as she'd wished a thousand times. He would say he was sorry, that he realized she was the one for him. They'd ride off into the sunset and live happily ever after.

The fairy tale ended with her next step and a dose of reality. She had no idea why Daniel was there. He could have come to apologize for his behavior, but not the outcome. He was the type to do just that, so she needed to put her expectations in a back drawer before she did herself more harm.

He turned when she was almost upon him. "Lisa."

She wasn't going to read anything into his breathlessness. "You're here."

He nodded.

"Did you call?" She opened her purse to get out her cell.

"No. I was afraid you wouldn't answer."

She looked at him again in the waning light. His hair was sticking up in a way that told her he'd run his hands through it a lot. His suit, normally impeccable, looked wrinkled. "How long have you been waiting?"

"Not long."

His breathing was coming fast, and the look of him…
"Do you want to come up, or are you in a hurry?"

"Yes. I mean, I'm not— I'd like to come up."

Her mouth had gone dry as they entered the building
and had gotten worse in the elevator. Not a word was spoken and they stood considerably farther apart than when
it'd been good. She hated that she was visibly shaking, but
she still managed to get them both inside. He turned to her
before she could close the door.

"I was an ass."

She inhaled. It was harder than ever to hold on to her
hopes. After shutting the door, she put her purse down on
the table. There were several envelopes in her in-box, all
with her real name, but that didn't matter now. "I asked a
lot of you the other night when I asked you to hear me out."

"I could have been more of a gentleman about it."

"Well, I'm not sure how this is going to turn out, but
go ahead. Say what you have to say." There was no way
she could hold back a small smile. He was there, with her.
And he wasn't angry. It made her feel better.

"I wanted you to know that some things have changed."
He wasn't quite meeting her eyes now, and although he'd
relaxed some, he started pacing, something he'd never done.
"For me, I mean. I'm going to start working full-time at
the Center in two weeks. I'll still volunteer at the clinic,
although I'll have limited hours. That should give me time
to see any non-emergency neurological cases. Emergency
cases will come right to the Center. I'll make sure they're
seen and treated, all pro bono. But only if it doesn't get
out of hand."

"Right." She should probably ask him to sit down. Or
why he was telling her all this. But all she could do was
stand there with her trembling hands and cautious heart.

He stopped in front of her. "Some things, some decisions, I'm not sure about. Not the things I needed to do, like step up at the Center. More personal things. But when I tried to think about my next step I…needed you."

She swallowed, warned herself not to get too excited. "Why?"

"Even when I was angry, I missed you so goddamn much. It drove me crazy. I've been a blind, self-righteous jerk. Finally, today, I was able to really understand all you'd told me." He let out a harsh breath. "I admit, Heather threw me. I should never have listened to her but we were still new, and I was confused about that damn trading card. But that's not important now. I owe you an apology for so much more."

"You're doing pretty well, I think."

He smiled. Took a half step forward. "It took me too long to figure out, but I finally get that when I took you to the cemetery I changed the rules. We were keeping things casual. Then I'd jumped ahead at least five big steps and I expected you to follow me when I had no right to."

"But I brought you here."

His brows came down and a sigh escaped. "I hadn't put that piece together."

"What do you mean?"

"I didn't understand what you meant about not talking about your client. I was dismissive, when I should have been respectful. I was also dismissive about something far more important." He lifted a hand, as though he wanted to touch her, and then lowered it to his side. "You know Eve and I go way back. We don't always agree on things. She's obstinate, and frankly annoying when she thinks she knows best. But even when I think she's off her rocker, I never, ever doubt she has my best interest at heart. She's the one who practically forced me into volunteering at

Moss Street. Not for as long as I was there, but it was her idea, and it was a good one. The point is if she ever betrayed me, I don't know what I'd do. I'd be adrift and broken. For a long time now she's been my compass. I can't know how it was for you when Tess betrayed you, but I think I understand how deep the wound is."

Lisa was shaking harder and for a completely different reason. When tears came she made no effort to stop them. "You're the only person who has."

He pulled her into his arms and kissed her. Then again, on her cheek where a tear had trailed. "I'm sorry," he whispered. Another kiss, as gentle as the first, on her neck, followed by "I'm sorry." More kisses, more apologies, until his lips rested on her collarbone, just as she stopped crying.

"Tell me how you missed me," she whispered. "Tell me—"

He straightened. "Every day I wrote you texts I didn't send. Every day I fought to stop needing you, but I lost every battle. I missed how you helped me realize I had possibilities. For years, I believed I either had to follow in my father's footsteps, or I wouldn't belong at the Center. It was you, watching you be braver than anyone I'd ever seen, going from nothing to a new life. You went out with me, when you hadn't dared in years. There aren't enough apologies for how I treated you, not after you stripped your soul bare when I was being such a prick."

She didn't know what to say. She hadn't even realized she was holding on to him so tightly there would be bruises on his shoulders. But he was holding her pretty damn tightly himself.

"You showed me how to ask for what I wanted, not what I thought I was allowed. You helped me realize I'm most definitely my own man, and I create the path I'm on. And..."

The way he looked at her, she thought he might kiss her again. Which would be wonderful. There was only one part of her dream that hadn't come true, and that was fine. She could be very happy with that. "Go ahead. No matter what you tell me…" She couldn't finish that sentence. Not yet.

Daniel smiled. "I also realized I love you."

The world stopped. Just for a second. But the most important second of her life.

"I'm in love with you," he whispered. "No matter what you feel right now, I needed to tell you that."

She blinked back to life. Back to him. "My name is Lisa Elizabeth McCabe, and I'm in love with you, Daniel Everett Cassidy."

The kiss that followed was pretty terrible, considering neither one of them could stop grinning. But they got into the spirit quickly. Especially after they'd migrated to her stupidly small bed.

Just after they sat, he said, "I don't want to rush you in any way."

"Too late."

He grinned but also shook his head. "Fair enough. Anyway, I thought you should know what I'm thinking, so there are no surprises later."

"Sounds reasonable. Aren't you hot in that suit?" She pushed his jacket off both shoulders, and then he shook it away, undeterred.

"I see us moving at your pace, but toward living together. No rush. I have no agenda about it, even though I'm going to ask your opinions about redecorating my house."

"No rush, though."

He cupped her cheek. "None. I mean it. If we just continue to date, and text, I'll be fine. If that works for you."

"I don't think you have to worry about that. I mean,

I'm not sure how fast I can go, but I've known for a while that the only future I can imagine is one with you in it."

He kissed her again. He just went for it, and she loved every second of his wild abandon. He had her blouse open before she took a very needed first breath, and unbuttoned his cuffs.

He grunted as he struggled to undo her bra while he kept kissing her.

"We should—" She forgot what she was going to say when he looked so amazingly perplexed. "One thing at a time," she said, most definitely not laughing.

He closed his eyes, and in a remarkably short time, she was down to her panties. They weren't even nice ones, but she didn't care. He then got down to business on his own clothes. "Oh, I also need help with decorating my office at the Center. It's hideous now."

"I thought everything in there was a priceless antique."

"Priceless doesn't mean they can't be ugly. Besides, they do have a price. From Sotheby's. I asked Warren what he wanted to do with them, and when I suggested an auction to help the clinic, he was fine with it."

He was on the bed now, straddling her hips. The fingers of his right hand were dipping underneath her panties. Not far enough—at least, not yet. "But I don't want to talk about that. The only thing that really matters to me right now is that I love you. And I see our road, with nothing written in stone. So many possibilities."

Lisa pulled him down for a kiss, happier than she'd ever been. "You *are* brilliant."

* * * * *

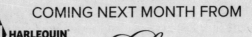
#847 MIDNIGHT THUNDER
Thunder Mountain Brotherhood
by Vicki Lewis Thompson
An emergency may have brought wandering cowboy
Cade Gallagher home, but the heat between him and former
flame Lexi Simmons is enough to keep him there. Lexi
isn't sure she trusts him, but she can't help give in to the
intense attraction...

#848 Fevered Nights
Uniformly Hot!
by Jillian Burns
Supermodel Piper Metcalf is trying to reform her bad-girl ways.
Just her luck she's met the only good guy who's trying to be
bad—sexy SEAL Neil Barrow. Will he be the one temptation she
can't turn down?

#849 COME ON OVER
Made in Montana
by Debbi Rawlins
Shelby Foster arrives at her inherited ranch desperate for a
fresh start. Too bad the Montana spread already has an
owner—seriously hot horse trainer Trent Kimball—and he is
not impressed!

#850 TRIPLE TIME
The Art of Seduction
by Regina Kyle
Straitlaced DA Gabe Nelson needs a friendlier image, and
bartender/artist Devin Padilla is happy to help him shake things
up. But their relationship turns more than friendly *fast*, and
opposites don't just attract—they get downright scorching.

REQUEST YOUR FREE BOOKS!
2 FREE NOVELS PLUS 2 FREE GIFTS!

HARLEQUIN®

Blaze®

red-hot reads!

YES! Please send me 2 FREE Harlequin® Blaze® novels and my 2 FREE gifts (gifts are worth about $10). After receiving them, if I don't wish to receive any more books, I can return the shipping statement marked "cancel." If I don't cancel, I will receive 4 brand-new novels every month and be billed just $4.74 per book in the U.S. or $5.21 per book in Canada. That's a savings of at least 14% off the cover price. It's quite a bargain. Shipping and handling is just 50¢ per book in the U.S. and 75¢ per book in Canada.* I understand that accepting the 2 free books and gifts places me under no obligation to buy anything. I can always return a shipment and cancel at any time. Even if I never buy another book, the two free books and gifts are mine to keep forever.

150/350 HDN GH2D

Name	(PLEASE PRINT)
Address	Apt. #
City	State/Prov. Zip/Postal Code

Signature (if under 18, a parent or guardian must sign)

Mail to the **Reader Service:**
IN U.S.A.: P.O. Box 1867, Buffalo, NY 14240-1867
IN CANADA: P.O. Box 609, Fort Erie, Ontario L2A 5X3

Want to try two free books from another line?
Call 1-800-873-8635 or visit www.ReaderService.com.

* Terms and prices subject to change without notice. Prices do not include applicable taxes. Sales tax applicable in N.Y. Canadian residents will be charged applicable taxes. Offer not valid in Quebec. This offer is limited to one order per household. Not valid for current subscribers to Harlequin Blaze books. All orders subject to credit approval. Credit or debit balances in a customer's account(s) may be offset by any other outstanding balance owed by or to the customer. Please allow 4 to 6 weeks for delivery. Offer available while quantities last.

Your Privacy—The Reader Service is committed to protecting your privacy. Our Privacy Policy is available online at www.ReaderService.com or upon request from the Reader Service.

We make a portion of our mailing list available to reputable third parties that offer products we believe may interest you. If you prefer that we not exchange your name with third parties, or if you wish to clarify or modify your communication preferences, please visit us at www.ReaderService.com/consumerchoice or write to us at Reader Service Preference Service, P.O. Box 9062, Buffalo, NY 14240-9062. Include your complete name and address.

HB15

SPECIAL EXCERPT FROM

H HARLEQUIN®

Blaze

*After years away, Cade Gallagher rushes back to
Thunder Mountain Ranch when he learns his foster
mom is in the hospital. But returning means facing his
past, and the woman he left behind…*

Read on for a sneak preview of
MIDNIGHT THUNDER,
the first book in
Vicki Lewis Thompson's
sexy new cowboy saga
THUNDER MOUNTAIN BROTHERHOOD.

"Thanks. This is great." Cade led Hematite into the stall, unhooked the lead rope and rubbed the horse's neck. "You're safe now, buddy. I'll be back to check on you in a few hours."

Hematite bumped his nose against Cade's arm. Then he walked over to the hay rack and began to munch.

Cade let out a breath as he left the stall and latched it behind him. While he coiled the lead rope, he gazed at the horse. "If I didn't know better, I'd think he understood what I just told him. I've never seen him so relaxed."

"At the very least, he probably picked up on your relief."

"I *am* relieved. I had no idea if this would work, if I could transport him from hell to heaven." He glanced at Lexi. "Thanks for making it possible."

She shrugged. "Don't thank me. I'm only doing what

He repositioned his hat in a typical Cade gesture. "They love to be of service, thank God. If they hadn't come along…"

Her heart squeezed. "I know."

"Yes, you do." He held her gaze. "You know that more than anyone. Lexi, I—"

"Go see Rosie." She wasn't ready for a heart-to-heart. "We're both tired. We'll talk later."

He nodded. "All right. But let me say this much. I've missed you every single day."

She swallowed her instinctive response. She'd missed him every single day, too, but she wasn't going to admit it. "Go see Rosie."

He turned as if to walk out of the barn. Then he swung back and reached for her. Before she could protest he'd pulled her into his arms and brought his mouth down on hers. It was a hard kiss, a kiss filled with frustration. There was no tenderness, only heat and confusion. It was over before she could respond.

He left the barn without looking back. Heart pounding, she pressed her fingers to her mouth. She still loved him with every fiber of her being. And he still loved her. But as she'd learned five years ago, love wasn't enough.

Don't miss
MIDNIGHT THUNDER by Vicki Lewis Thompson,
available in June 2015 wherever
Harlequin® Blaze® books and ebooks are sold.

WITH *Romance*

Harlequin has everything from contemporary, passionate and heartwarming to suspenseful and inspirational stories.

Whatever your mood, we have a romance just for you!

Connect with us to find your next great read, special offers and more.

f /HarlequinBooks

🐦 @HarlequinBooks

www.HarlequinBlog.com

www.Harlequin.com/Newsletters

⟨H⟩ HARLEQUIN®

A *Romance* FOR EVERY MOOD™

www.Harlequin.com